CRUISING FOR LOVE

CRUISING FOR LOVE

•

Tami Cowden

AVALON BOOKS
NEW YORK

PRINTED IN THE UNITED STATES OF AMERICA
ON ACID-FREE PAPER
BY HADDON CRAFTSMEN, BLOOMSBURG, PENNSYLVANIA

For my very own Steve, the hero of my personal
story, who always encourages me to
partake of life's banquets.

And for Caro and Sue, who taught me to ask "why?"

Everlasting appreciation goes to the staff and members of Romance Writers of America, an organization that does much to help writers achieve and continue their success, and to the members of the Colorado Romance Writers and Heart of Denver Romance Writers, who have given me ceaseless inspiration and motivation.

My thanks also go to Angi, Linda, Kassia, Jill, Jenn, and Paula, for helping to make this business fun.

Chapter One

He was the answer to her prayers.

That is, if prayers for help in perpetuating lies were answered. Nina Kerensky mulled that theological issue for only an instant as she stared at the hunk replacing her retiring veterinarian.

Unbelievable. He fit the description she had given Grams perfectly. Tall, dark hair, gray eyes, lean muscular build. She had to be dreaming this.

With a start, she realized he was speaking.

"Pleased to meet you, Ma'am,"

Was that just a touch of Texas in his voice? Her imaginary husband Steve spoke with just such a drawl.

Rendered speechless at the miracle in cowboy boots standing in front of her, she could only nod and hold out a shaking hand for his firm warm grasp. But reaching out that hand left her grasp on the cat carrier in her arms unbalanced. Accompanied by the snarling sound of a grumpy Russian Blue cat, the carrier slipped toward the floor.

"Whoa, there!" The solution to all her problems had quick reflexes. He saved Sasha from an ignominious dumping. "Here you go, Ms. Kerensky." He righted the carrier, and made soothing sounds to her cat. "Let me help bring her to the counter here."

"Thank you, Dr. Tabor." Still dazed at her good fortune, she followed him to the receptionist's window. She noted the care with which he set the carrier down with vague approval as she pondered how to put her proposition to him.

"Call me Steve, Ma'am." He grinned, revealing wide, even teeth, and winked. "Dr. Tabor was my mother."

His name was Steve? Nina looked warily around the waiting room. These coincidences were getting a little too spooky. But then again, who was she to look a gift horse in the mouth?

Her mind finally registered his last words. "Your mother was a veterinarian too?" Being an animal doctor seemed like an arduous career for a family woman.

"She still is. In West Texas."

Texas? If he was from Texas, he must not be a member of the fabulously wealthy Tabor family. Owners of a few sports franchises in Denver, the family was a longtime Colorado institution. "Was your father a vet too?" She wondered if, like hers, his parents had met through their careers.

"No, not my father." Laughter filled the gray eyes. "He doesn't have much use for animals. Unless they're running a race."

She blinked at that, but further inquiry was cut short by the approach of her soon-to-retire vet, Dr. Williams.

"I see you've met my successor, Nina." The deep lines around his eyes crinkled merrily as he patted Steve on the back. "It was quite a coup for me to get young Steve to come to Denver to take over for me. On his mother's side, his people have been vets for generations. The best in Texas." He gave a happy sigh. "I can retire with an easy mind now, knowing all my patients will be in good hands."

Nina's eyes were drawn to those good hands, currently engaged in stroking Sasha's glossy gray fur. Long tanned fingers promised dexterity.

A surgeon's hands! Even as her heart skipped a beat at her good luck, she made a mental note of the total absence of any rings on the left hand.

"Yes, Steve here will do a great job."

"I'll do my best, sir." Beneath his browned face, a faint flush colored his face. Modest, too. She liked that in a guy.

Of course, it was just too good to be true. His perfection for the role was just divine punishment for her lies. He couldn't possibly be available on such short notice.

Still, she had to ask.

"When do you start, Steve?"

"In two weeks."

"Not for two weeks! That's, that's terrific. Two weeks! Wonderful—" She stopped in the middle of her excited exclamation when she noticed two sets of eyebrows raised high over two pairs of eyes.

She sighed. She saw that expression a lot.

She suspected the same look would be plastered on Steve's face when she asked him to accompany her on a cruise. It would stay there as he laughed in her face and told her to face the consequences of her actions.

She didn't even want to think about what sweet, kindly Dr. William's reaction to her tangle of lies would be.

Exaggerations, not lies. It had all started with just a bit of exaggeration about meeting a man in Europe. Somehow, that tiny exaggeration had turned into a full-fledged husband who had to be at her side on a cruise tomorrow, or Grams' heart would break. And Nina's with it.

She took a deep breath to fortify herself for her tale of woe.

The door burst open suddenly as a woman with two Dalmatians straining against their leashes entered the waiting room. Sasha did not take kindly to their intrusion. It was several minutes before the resulting commotion had quieted. By the time the cat had been coaxed into a more compliant disposition, and the dogs hustled into an examination room, Nina realized Steve had walked out into the parking lot.

He's leaving?

"Hey! Wait up a second!" She ran to the door. She threw a hurried "I'll be right back" over her shoulder to the receptionist whose work space was now filled with disgruntled gray cats.

"Steve, please wait!"

He stopped at the sound of her call and walked back

to the sidewalk in front of the office. "Yes, Ms. Kerensky? Is there something I can help you with?"

His professional smile actually reached his eyes. She liked that.

"Call me Nina, and oh, boy, is there ever." She stopped, realizing that asking a perfect—and he *was* perfect—stranger to go off on a cruise with her could seem a little forward. She squinted against the bright midday sun to look up into his face. Her hands waved in circles in front of her as she tried to find the right words.

"Did I hear right? You aren't actually starting to work at "Best for Pets" for two weeks?" She tried not to stare at the long black lashes surrounding his wide gray eyes. The color was cool, yet she felt warmed.

"Yes, you heard right. Dr. Williams begins his retirement in two weeks. I take over then."

"Great!"

"I see." His eyes narrowed a bit, darkening to flint. He stood a little straighter, and said stiffly, "Ms. Kerensky, if you are concerned about the care I would give Sasha, I assure you I am fully qualified. Besides helping my mother every time I was with her, I had my own practice for several years."

"Oh, no." Her mouth dropped with dismay at his misunderstanding. Some vets didn't seem to like animals much, but she could tell he did. After all, he'd even remembered her cat's name. "No, I'm sure you'll do great."

The flint softened a bit, and she forged ahead. "I was just wondering if, if you had any plans for those two weeks?" She ended in a rush, as heat rose to her cheeks, "'Cause if you didn't, I have a proposition for you."

She had never, in her life, issued a proposition to a man before. Not even one she was dating, let alone someone she'd just met. Of course, she wasn't making *that* kind of proposition. But the stunned look on his face told her what he thought.

"Well, I guess people don't waste much time around these parts, do they?" His head shook with apparent bemusement as he looked her up and down. "That's a right generous offer, Ma'am."

She felt her own flush deepen under his assessment, although she could not help the tiny tingle of pleasure running along her spine at his approval. Glancing again at his sun-browned hands, she had to admit she couldn't think of anyone better suited for that kind of proposition.

Frowning, Nina shook her head slightly to clear it of such distracting thoughts.

"Uh, that's not what. Uh, I mean, what I need is a husband. Not a one night stand."

If anything, his eyes got wider. He put his hands up as though to ward her off, as he backed up a few steps.

"Sorry, lady, but I've been out of the husband business for almost six months now."

The grimness underscoring his words told her there was a story there somewhere. But his feelings toward marriage weren't a problem. Heck, she shared them. So she hastened to reassure him. "Oh, not a real husband, just for pretend. For just one week." Adopting a wheedling tone, she added, "To make a sweet old lady happy."

The desperate note in her voice seemed to add to his conviction that she was a lunatic. He backed up another step and glanced up and down the sidewalk as though for help.

"Look, I know this sounds crazy." She scowled at his nod. "But there is a perfectly rational explanation."

His brows lifted, but he said nothing.

"You see, my grandmother is surprising me. I mean, she's not really, she just thinks she is. My sister Ana warned me, though. She's coming on the cruise too. I mean, I'm a travel writer, and I have this assignment." She stopped in the face of the dazed look settling on his. "Oh! The thing is, it's a long story."

"Yeah, it would have to be, wouldn't it?" He quirked an eyebrow at her, apparently no longer worried that she was batty. "I mean, for a woman to go soliciting strangers to marry her, there'd have to be a long story, wouldn't there?"

She bristled. Why did no one ever take her seriously?

"Look, I'm not asking you to marry me. I just want you to be my husband for one week. You don't need to act like I'm asking you to do something illegal or anything." The justification for his ridicule didn't make his attitude any less irritating.

But reality was bringing her down from the high flights of her fantasy. Realizing she'd have go back to her first plan to tell Grams the truth, her hopes sank to her toes. She studied those toes peeping out of the sexy sandals she had bought for the trip as she shuddered at the disappointment she would cause.

Forlornly, she made a last ditch effort. "Are you sure you wouldn't like a free cruise?"

"A free cruise?" Amused disbelief rang true and clear in his voice.

But his question did indicate *some* interest. And that was enough to keep her in the game.

"Look, just let me get Sasha settled, and I'll explain everything. Over coffee?" She nodded toward the coffee shop next to "Best for Pets." She started trotting back to the vet's office as she said again. "I'll explain everything."

"Hey!" Steve stared at the rapidly retreating back of the most unusual woman he'd ever met. Her wildly colored skirt billowed out at the ends, revealing shapely long legs.

"How do they find me?" he mused. He looked toward his car, wondering if a wise man wouldn't simply take off before the redheaded nut came back. But he was heading for the coffeehouse before he'd even completed the thought.

Wisdom never had been his strong suit.

Besides, he couldn't help but feel intrigued by a woman who thought a free cruise would appeal to a member of the Tabor family. In fact, he wasn't entirely sure his family didn't own a cruise line.

A few minutes later, all eyes in the quiet shop turned to the door as it burst open. And no wonder. The lady was definitely worth a good long look.

Nina stood in the entrance, scanning the tables. She was outlined by sunlight, her trim form revealed through the gauzy cloth of her skirt. In the afternoon light, her hair took on a coppery fire tone as it billowed down to her shoulders.

He told himself the sweat breaking out on his upper lip was entirely due to the scalding black coffee he was drinking.

A brilliant smile lit her face as she saw him. Against his will, he felt an answering smile snake across his own mouth. He rose when she approached his table and pulled out a chair.

"I was worried you wouldn't be here," she confided over her shoulder as he helped her into her seat.

"Not sure why I am." He returned to his own place and winced as the spindly café chair pressed against his lower back. It wasn't meant for a man of his height. He took another gulp of his coffee.

"I'll have a double-tall, half no-fat, mocha latte, with chocolate sprinkles." She grinned at the waitress, and tossed the ends of that silky red hair back over her shoulder.

Then she turned that dazzling smile on him.

"I'm guessing you never get decaf." Even sitting down, she radiated energy.

"Oh, no," she said as she tapped her fingertips against the table. "Caffeine never affects me."

He watched in skeptical silence as she fiddled with the items on the table, straightened the napkin holder, and turned all the sweetener packets right side up. Finally, her coffee arrived, and she took a deep swallow.

"So, why does a nice girl like you need a husband in a hurry?" He looked closely at her slim body, noting her full bosom. Just the right size, he thought, tightening his grip on his cup. But no thickened waist, or fullness in her face to suggest a baby on the way. "You don't look pregnant."

She choked on her drink. After a few coughs, she sputtered, "Of course, I'm not having a baby. How foolish do you think I am?"

He opened his mouth to speak, but she forestalled him with a slim, elegant finger, its glossy pink-tipped nail pointed right at his nose. "Don't answer that!"

He couldn't help but smile at her indignation. She looked very cute, her green eyes darkening as she glowered at him. She pursed rosy lips and cocked her head.

He licked his own lips, wondering what hers tasted like.

She waggled the finger at him, but apparently thought better of the action, because she sat back in her seat and laughed.

"Okay. I've been living with this situation so long that it doesn't seem all that strange to me anymore. When the whole thing developed, it seemed so reasonable. So harmless." After a heavy sigh, she continued. "But I'll admit that I must seem a bit, well, odd to you, approaching you like this."

Odd. Warning bells went off in his head at the sound of that word. That was his problem, he was too attracted to the out-of-the-ordinary types. Especially when they needed help.

But even though this lady was adding up to be a bit

too much like his unlamented ex, Sandra, he couldn't help himself. He had to know what the problem was.

"Why don't you just tell it to me from the beginning?"

"From the beginning." Another sigh. "All right. My parents were Olympic skaters, you see—" She broke off at his stifled exclamation. "What?"

He cast a harried look around the coffee shop. "Uh, maybe you should start the explanation a little closer to the present situation. Cut to the chase."

"Oh. Sure." She frowned in concentration. "The chase. Um, let's see." She took a deep breath, presenting an opportunity for him to view the creamy skin swelling out from the top of her blouse. But her words soon snapped his attention back to her face. "I told my grandmother I married a doctor named Steve, and that we are going on a cruise tomorrow for a belated honeymoon. So my grandmother decided to surprise me with a mini-family reunion. So she and my sister Ana are coming on the cruise too. That way, they can finally meet my husband."

His jaw dropped. Shaking his head, he managed to ask, "If your grandmother's reunion idea is a surprise, how come you know about it?"

"My sister let it slip. She's a sports photographer and mentioned that she'll be missing an important event because of the cruise. I dragged the whole plan out of her." She took a dainty swallow of her coffee. "So, anyway, I need to find a doctor named Steve to go on the cruise with me, or else I have to break the heart of my sweet seventy-year-old grandmother by telling her that I've been lying to her for months." She had been staring at her lap as she recounted her deception, but now she looked earnestly up at him, her green eyes filled with entreaty. "So, if you aren't doing anything else, it's a great cruise. Lots of terrific scenery."

How could such an accomplished liar possibly have such innocent eyes? Such a pure smile? And wasn't she just what he needed? Another gorgeous liar.

"But I'm a veterinarian, not a doctor." Hearing his own words, Steve sat up. After that outrageous story, that ridiculous scheme, the only objection he could come up with was his own lack of qualifications? What was wrong with him? He had to keep his thinking above the waistline.

"Oh, but that doesn't matter." She brushed this obstacle aside breezily. "You must know enough to *sound* like a doctor. I mean, no one is going to ask you to perform surgery on a *person* or anything."

There had to be more to this than a plan to make a grandmother happy. Was there some sort of stupid inheritance at stake? Was she trying to win a bet? Was she just a pathological liar? His curiosity got the better of his good sense telling him to hightail it out of there. He asked, "Why'd you tell your grandmother you were married in the first place?"

Her long sigh blew a wisp of red hair flying up. "Because she wants me to be married."

He cocked his head at her and waited. When she simply smiled back at him, he prompted, "And why does she want that?"

"Oh, well." She shrugged, distracting him momentarily with a tiny peek at the gentle curve at the bodice of her loose blouse. "You see, Grams thinks women can only be happy if they're married and have kids." The beautiful face turned tragic. "She thinks I am throwing my chances away by traveling all over and never staying put long enough to meet any men. She doesn't understand I'm not cut out to be Suzy Homemaker."

No, this free spirit definitely didn't look like a '50s housewife type. But then again, what woman did nowadays? For that matter, what man wanted a woman obsessed with homemaking?

On the other hand, he certainly understood families who got upset when their expectations weren't met. His father still couldn't get over having a son who threw away his chance at Olympic gold and his brother considered him an embarrassment because he actually worked. "So your grandmother hoped you'd meet a rich doctor and become one of the ladies that lunch? Like her?"

She chuckled. "Well, that's not exactly Grams's style. No, she and Gramps were both teachers. And when Gramps passed away and she retired from teaching, she started selling her paintings, so it's not that she doesn't think I should have some kind of a career. She just doesn't understand that I need my freedom. That I love writing about all the places in the world to see and all the things to do. That I need to experience life at its fullest."

Oh. A party girl. "You want to go for the gusto, huh?" How many times had Sandra said words to that effect to him? How many times had she looked for gusto in some other guy's bedroom?

"Hey, I want to live my own life, and realize my own dreams, not just watch my husband live his. But I don't want to hurt Grams, either." She stared into the depths of her milky coffee drink. "So, anyway, when I was in Innsbruck last August, Grams got sick. I wanted to come home, but she said no, and started talking about how romantic it was that I was in the city where my parents met and married and how she'd be so happy if the same thing happened to me." She looked at him, catching him once again with those deep green eyes. "My parents were figure skaters, you see. They met at a competition."

"Why were you in Innsbruck?"

"Oh, for my column. 'The Solitary Traveler.' Innsbruck is a great destination. You really get a sense of old Europe there." She took another sip of her drink, leaving a faint spot of cream at the edge of her full lips, right next to a tiny beauty mark.

He licked his own lips again. It took every ounce of his strength to keep from leaning over, and lapping the cream from her mouth.

"Have you read it?"

The movement of her mouth clued him in to her question. His gaze lifted from the tantalizing juxtaposition of the cream and beauty mark.

"I'm sorry, what did you ask?"

"My column? 'The Solitary Traveler?' Have you ever read it? It's in a lot of papers, including the *Post*.

He shook his head, resisting an urge to run over and grab a paper. The huge eyes looked down at her drink again.

"Well, anyway, with Grams sick and all, I sort of just made up this guy to make her feel better. And she perked right up, and got better, so I just kept talking about how well the relationship was going, and before I knew it, Steve and I had eloped."

Okay, that got his full attention. She had eloped with an imaginary guy before she knew it? The lady obviously had an imagination on overdrive. The voice in his head telling him to get out of Dodge raised the volume a notch. But he stuck around long enough to ask, "So this was nearly a year ago? How could you keep the lie up all this time?"

"Well, I said Steve was a surgeon, to explain why he was always so busy. His schedule kept him from coming on my last visit to Grams and Ana with me. And I really did have lots of trips to make for my writing, so there was no point in her visiting us. I mean, visiting me." Her shoulders slumped as she sat back in the chair. "But then Grams started worrying about how little time Steve and I spend together, and that was no way to conduct a marriage. So I told her he's coming on this cruise with me so we could finally take a honeymoon." She glanced up at him. "'Cause we never did, you see."

"Kind of ironic, don't you think, a travel writer not getting to go on a honeymoon?" He wondered if that ever occurred to this grandmother of hers.

Nina cocked her head at that, rather struck. "I guess it is ironic, at that." She shrugged. "But some would say we already had the honeymoon. In Innsbruck."

An amazingly pragmatic view from someone with her imagination. He shook his head in amazement at the contradictions in her. The lady was definitely a nut-case. He opened his mouth to refuse her request.

But then she looked up into his eyes, and reached across the coffee cups to lay her hand on his forearm. "Please, Steve. Please help me from breaking Grams' heart."

At her touch, his arm, and then the rest of him, flooded with heat. In fact, the temperature seemed to be so high in this place, he wondered if steam was flowing from his ears.

He wet his lips, trying to tear his gaze from those emerald eyes. "This is insane. Just tell your grandmother the truth."

"But she'll be devastated. She was so happy when I told her we had gotten married. And she had been feeling kind of sick again, but when I told her about the wedding, she got better right away. Besides, she understood perfectly that your surgery schedule made it impossible to take time off to visit with me."

"My surgery schedule?" His voice sounded a bit strangled to his own ears, which was easy to understand. He was having trouble catching his breath.

"Well, you know. Steve the doctor's schedule." She straightened her shoulders. "Look, I know it sounds kind of crazy, but here's the deal. If you come on this cruise, and pretend to be my husband, I'll pay for the whole thing."

Like he cared about the cost. He tried to stop her flow of words, but she kept right on speaking.

"I'm a travel writer, so I have tons of frequent flyer miles. The flight to the port will be no problem. And I already have a cabin with two beds, so I'm sure it won't be a problem to get another ticket. I get a terrific discount."

His brow rose. They'd be rooming together? Her reference to two beds made it clear that sleeping arrangements would be separate, but sharing a cabin had potential. The lady's *proposition* was starting to sound rather attractive.

"Yes, first class the whole way. Well, no, not first class, exactly. Tourist class, in fact, but the cabin's just for sleeping, anyway." She continued her eager description of the delights awaiting him. Those offered by the ship, anyway. Swimming, golf, casino gambling.

He studied her animated face as she enthusiastically told him of all the amenities. She exuded innocence, despite her obvious flair for lying. Was she aware of the implications of her offer? Would she find some other guy to fill in if he refused? He pictured her with someone else. Someone she just picked up at an office, on the street. Maybe even someone in this coffee shop.

He glanced around. The café was filled with ordinary people, dressed in business suits or casual street clothes. No one looked like an ax murderer. But then again, homicidal maniacs look just like everyone else.

Did she know there were a lot of crazies out there? She could get hurt.

He could go. There was nothing keeping him in Denver until his job started. He really didn't want to hang out at Dad's place. Heck, his own furniture wouldn't even arrive for another ten days, so he was stuck using a sleeping bag on an inflatable mattress in his new apartment.

Sharing a cabin. His temperature shot up another degree at the thought of being in such close quarters with the bubbly female seated before him. He thought of her body in a bikini, cavorting in a sun-dappled pool.

A cruise? Where had she said it was going? He'd been too stunned by the invitation to hear. But a cruise meant hot tropical nights and exotic drinks, right?

The Caribbean? Or the Mexican Riviera? Did it even matter? Either way, there'd be this redhead in a bikini.

He realized she was still selling the fun of a cruise.

"—a really great cruise line. Terrific food, fantastic events. Lots of fun stops and exciting shore tour possibilities. I have a brochure in my car, if you want to see it."

"Yeah, yeah, sounds great." He nodded distractedly. He pushed images of sharing a hammock on the beach out of his head to deal with practical matters. "I don't understand why you have to go to these lengths. If you can't tell your grandmother the truth, why don't you just cancel the trip. Blame it on my, I mean, on Steve the doctor's, surgery schedule."

"Can't do it. I have to go on that cruise." Her head shook sadly. "This is my big chance for a feature in *21st Century Traveling*. If the editor likes the story, I might end up a regular columnist. But if I can't turn in that article, the editor will probably never even look at a proposal from me again, let alone consider me for the full time spot. I can't afford to take that risk."

She turned on her pleading look again. This lady had the most expressive face he'd ever seen. A guy would have to be made of stone to resist that look.

He wasn't made of stone.

Hold it! No way did he need to get involved with another beautiful liar. Hooking up, even for pretend, with a lady with this much freedom with facts, was not the way to start his new life back here in Denver. He was supposed to be getting far away from the scheming gold diggers of Texas. It was certainly a nice change to be offered a free trip, instead of hearing hints he should be arranging yet another one, but still, she was an admitted liar.

"Sorry, Nina—Ms. Kerensky. But I can't help you." Forcing himself to look away from the dejection written on her face, he pulled out his wallet to remove some bills to pay the tab.

"No, no. The coffee was on me." Elbow on the table, she propped her cheek on one hand as she waved away his money with the other. A heavy sigh escaped her, sending that tantalizing lock of hair flying up again. "Anyway, thanks for listening. I really hope you like your new job."

He couldn't recall a woman ever turning down an offer for him to foot the bill, no matter how small. Her reluctance to accept even the price of a coffee made him feel like a heel. That she had to be nice enough to wish him luck on the job made him feel even lower.

Jeez, why should he feel bad for not agreeing to play along with a pack of lies? Knowing if he stayed a single instant longer, he'd give in, he strode off without saying another word.

Walking away was the right thing to do. He'd be nuts to get involved with a scheme like this. And besides, the redhead did things to him. Even now, just having spent a few minutes with her, he was tingling.

Tingling? He stopped in the middle of the parking lot. Can't blame that on the redhead. His cell phone was vibrating. His good sense still arguing with his compassion, he flipped it opened absently. "Steve Tabor."

"Steve, darling! How are you?" The southern lilt of his ex-wife brought him to a halt.

He sighed. "How much, Sandra?" A call from her always heralded a request for money. He preferred to live on his own earnings, but at times he took a certain perverse pleasure in throwing some of his family's nearly ill-gotten gains away on his ex. After all, his father thought Sandra, a bronze medalist swimmer, was such an appropriate bride for a member of the Tabor family and its sports dynasty.

If bed hopping were a competitive sport, Sandra would have taken the gold for sure.

"Oh, Steve, how unkind. I am not calling to ask you for money." The trilling laugh he'd found sexy once upon a time slammed into his ear.

"No money, huh?" He made no effort to keep the skepticism out of his voice. "What, then?"

"Well, there's something you need to know. Something you need to hear in person. But I can tell you this. I'm moving to Denver."

"You hate Denver."

"Well, I hated Dallas too. Denver's no worse." Rare candor laced through her tone before she returned to the sugary sweet attitude he'd grown to hate. "But a woman does strange things for love, honey."

Remembering the exact position in which he'd found her and his former best friend, Rick Andrews, he had to agree with that statement. But how would love bring her to Denver? Andrews didn't live here. A sudden thought stopped him in his tracks. "Sandra, you don't have some crazy idea of getting back together with me, do you?"

Another laugh trilled across the microwaves. "Of course not, darling. Nothing could be farther from the truth. In fact—well, actually, it's a surprise. I promised I wouldn't tell you. He doesn't want to yet, anyway."

Relief swept through him at her denial. "I can't think of anything important you'd have to say to me."

"Steven, don't be difficult. It's important. The truth is . . ."

He sighed. Sandra loved stopping in the middle of sentences for what she thought was dramatic effect. Her idea of high drama was watching Captain Kirk on old Star Trek episodes.

". . . I'm getting married again."

Married? "What kind of idiot—" He cut off his instinctive, albeit rather rude, response. And he was no one to judge another man. After all, he'd been exactly that kind of idiot once upon a time.

Anyway, he knew who it had to be. "Don't bother to tell me who. I can guess." He supposed he should at least be glad his old buddy Andrews actually cared enough for Sandra to marry her. That ought to take some of the sting from the betrayal.

Still, he couldn't help but be surprised his friend had marriage in mind, but then, Sandra always had a way of keeping men from thinking straight.

"You can?" A pause. "Well, what do you think?" Wariness outweighed her usual seductive tone.

"I think you deserve each other. But it's not my business."

"But it is, dear. We don't want you to be unhappy about this. Especially since we'll be living right there in Denver. At least, some of the time. So we'll meet and have dinner."

"No, thanks." Cripes, like he'd want to go out with his ex-wife and the two-faced friend with whom she'd betrayed him. In fact, the only thing that brought him back to Denver was the knowledge that here, at least, he didn't run the risk of meeting up with someone who'd slept with his wife.

Not much of one, anyway. Maybe.

But now she was coming here? Colorado would never know what hit it. "So when does the invasion take place?"

"We're flying in tomorrow. I've taken a whole floor at the Brown Palace and we're having a huge party to announce our engagement."

"Leave me off the guest list, Sandra. I won't be coming to any parties." He stated the words flatly.

"Don't be silly. It would ruin everything if you act like you're jealous." He could hear the triumph in her voice. She just could not believe he'd been happy to be rid of her. He knew she told anyone who would listen that he had begged her not to leave him.

So now if he didn't show up at this party, everyone would believe he was nursing a broken heart. In the local paper, the society columnist would snicker about all the rumors from the divorce, while the sports columnist would dredge up his opting out of the competition years ago. He didn't really care about anyone's opinion, but the inevitable result would be questions in the eyes of everyone who knew him. Just the sort of thing he'd grown to hate in Dallas.

Of course, no one would expect him to smile at an engagement party if he really had other plans. Plans that at least looked long-term. Besides, if there was one excuse for missing an event the high society crowd accepted, it was having a better offer. He glanced back at the coffee house.

All of a sudden, the common sense that had told him to walk away from the redhead was singing a different tune. Sunshine, tropical ocean breezes, a bit of relaxation before he took over for Dr. Williams. Just what he needed. Heck, even the sports hacks would agree that fun in the sun with a gorgeous redhead should not be passed up. "Sorry, Sandra, but the gloating party will have to carry on without me. I'm taking a cruise. And I leave tomorrow."

"A cruise? What are you talking about?" Apparently she was so surprised she didn't even bother to maintain her usual sultry tone.

"A cruise. You know. A big boat filled with people having fun."

"A cruise where?" Disbelief rang loud and clear across the phone connection.

Steve frowned. Where exactly had the redhead said it was going? She'd told him about it, but he'd been too startled by her fake marriage proposal to pay attention.

"The Bahamas? Or Caribbean. Somewhere like that."

"You don't even know where the ship is going? Honestly, Steve, if you are going to make up improbable lies, you should at least put some thought into them."

"Like you, huh? Been to any bachelorette parties lately?" He certainly remembered her excuse for heading out on the town one night. Too bad he'd already known the couple had broken up two weeks before.

"Steve, darling, this is exactly why we need to meet and talk things over. Just think how uncomfortable family parties will be if you are still carrying a torch for me."

He resisted the temptation to throw the phone across the parking lot. "Family parties? Yeah, like you and Rick will be invited."

"But—"

"Get over yourself, Sandra. I don't care where the damn boat is going. I'm taking a cruise with a gorgeous redhead." A flick of the "end" button cut off Sandra's surprised exclamations. With a few quick strides, he was back in the coffeehouse.

Nina was still sitting at the table, her eyes downcast. With one pale pink fingertip, she slowly traced a pattern in the table's marble top. He flung himself down opposite her and savored the astonishment in her ocean green eyes.

"I've changed my mind. When does the loveboat leave?"

Chapter Two

Steve let his tense muscles relax a bit as he eased down next to Nina in the cab. One more stop and then they were off to the airport.

He'd known he would regret his impulsive decision to help out the pretty fibber. He just hadn't counted on regretting it before they'd even gotten on the plane.

Getting ready for this little cruise trip had been a trip in itself.

He already had a passport, so that was okay.

And clothes hadn't been too much of a problem. The sweet little lady next to him had turned into a fireball at his reluctance to buy swimming trunks. Cut-offs had always been fine in the family pool, but she had been quite indignant at the very thought. In the end, he had given in.

Nonetheless, he had stood firm on the issue of a tuxedo. Withstanding first the flashing green fire shooting from her eyes, and then, when she'd tried another tack, a heartstring-pulling pout, he'd resisted all attempts to force him into a monkey suit. If he'd wanted to play the social scene, he could stay home. He hadn't bothered to bring his tux when he'd moved to Colorado, and he wasn't going to let Nina buy him another.

But there had been no escape when it came to the required immunizations. Nina said if he didn't have them, they wouldn't let him off the dock.

He hated shots. No problem giving them, but getting them was another story.

They'd had to call all over Denver to find a medical facility willing to give him four shots without making an appointment six weeks in advance. He'd finally had to pull in a favor from an old sports doctor from his college days. He rubbed the sore spot on his arm in remembrance.

"Does it still hurt?" Her soft voice held equal measures of sympathy and guilt.

His arm did still hurt, as did another location. Quite a bit. As if getting all those shots at once weren't bad enough, the harried nurse had broken a needle in him for the last one. They had gotten it out, but the experience had cost him an ounce or two of flesh. And that shot hadn't been in his arm.

"It's more the memory of the experience."

"Well, it's over now." She gave him that smile of hers again. "The nurse didn't mean to hurt you. The poor woman had to give you four shots in a row, so she was bound to get tired."

He snorted. Well, if that didn't just figure. Her concern was for the nurse.

"That 'poor woman' went to school for years to learn how to do her job right."

"That's true. But I'm just saying there was no call for you to grab the hypodermic away from the nurse and give yourself the shot. She felt bad about things already."

"I made *her* feel bad?" He shook his head. "Sheesh. I was the one who'd had a piece of metal dug out of my—out of me. How about a little sympathy for me?"

Nina's lush pink lips rounded into an "O" and compassion filled her wide sea green eyes. "Oh, it really does hurt you, doesn't it?" She leaned toward him across the seat of the cab to pat his hand. "I'm so very sorry."

His indignation slipped as a smooth expanse of neckline was revealed.

"It's not so bad." His words were gruffer than he'd intended. While he rather liked the feeling of being on the receiving end of a woman's compassion, he never had been good at admitting pain.

She started to straighten, taking the tantalizing view away.

"It hurts!"

She leaned closer to him, concern written all over her face.

And he looked at her face. He did, for a whole second or two, before dropping his gaze again to the gentle swell peeking from beneath her lacy blouse. Today's wispy top was a creamy white color, the perfect emphasis for a tan that, as far as he could tell from his line of vision, did not stop.

He licked his suddenly dry lips. Immediately, he began to imagine the view if the lacy thing suddenly disappeared.

Thoughts like that are what got you four shots, Stevie boy.

But right now, as he inhaled her subtle jasmine scent, the needle pricks suddenly seemed like a small price to pay for the opportunity to spend seven days in a ship's cabin with her. A small cabin, he hoped. A tiny cabin.

With a double bed instead of twins. He let the fantasy continue for a few minutes.

"Here you go, folks." The cab driver pulled up next to a large windowless building. A huge sign claimed the large chain discount jewelry store was their "FRIEND IN THE DIAMOND BUSINESS."

"Hey, we're here already!" She bounced on her seat with excitement. "We'll get the wedding rings, and then we're off to the wide blue yonder." She pursed generous pink lips and shook her head. "I still can't believe none of my married friends would loan their rings for a week."

"Some people are so selfish." He laughed as he opened the door and helped her out of the cab. Her air of cheerful innocence was a delight. "Might as well look the part," he said, holding out his arm with a jaunty air. His sore arm, he realized too late, as Nina gaily latched on to it. Holding back a wince, he let himself be pulled after his sashaying partner.

Their friends in the diamond business were indeed

very friendly. The showroom fairly burst with sales clerks standing by brilliantly lit display cases. A polished-looking young man approached them immediately.

"Hello, I'm David. How may I be of service to you?" He smiled broadly, causing Steve to squint at the expanse of white teeth he showed. "And may I say what a lovely couple you make?"

Steve snorted at this practiced effusiveness, but Nina seemed happy enough with the cliché.

"We'd like to see some wedding rings, please." She returned the salesman's smile in full force, causing a blink on the latter's part. But the professional's recovery came quicker than Steve's had.

"Of course, of course, best wishes to you both." He clasped his hands together gleefully as he led them to a display case. "And an engagement ring for the lady?" He nodded meaningfully at Nina's bare left hand.

"Oh, no. We just need wedding rings." Her head turned this way and that, as she tried to decide which display case to examine first. "We're not getting engaged."

The puzzlement passed across the clerk's eyes so quickly, Steve couldn't swear he'd seen it. But he could sure see the half-reproachful, half-contemptuous look he was getting now. The salesman's thoughts were coming through loud and clear. He might just as well have shouted to the whole display room "this guy is too cheap to buy his lady a diamond."

A hot flush climbed Steve's neck. He glanced around

the showroom, half expecting to see derisive looks on every customer.

But despite the dirty look, the clerk merely said, "Pity. A solitaire would be perfect for the shape of your hand, Miss."

Steve stared at her hand. Soft, smooth, her fingers were long and well-shaped. A diamond would indeed look good on her hand.

Don't be an idiot. Of course a jewelry salesman wants her to have a diamond if it means he gets the commission. Who cares what he thinks? Despite that thought, he heard himself say, "We want to look at engagement rings too."

Darn. That proved it. Nina was officially making him crazy.

"No, we don't." Nina looked at him as though he'd lost his mind.

Well, hadn't he? Why else would he be participating in this harebrained scheme?

"Just a wedding band. That's all we need." Her voice was loud enough to cause heads to turn their way. A blue-haired lady tilted back her head so she could look down her nose at him. Nina didn't bother to lower her voice when she added to him, "I don't want a diamond ring. I can't afford it." The old woman's eyes widened before she sniffed and turned away in disgust.

His eyes closed briefly as he felt the impact of her revelation about footing the bill hit the other customers. He suspected botanists would kill to have tomatoes as red as his face must be. He glanced at the source of whispers in the corner of the showroom. A large man in a Denver Bronco's cap sneered at him before proclaiming, "I saved for five years to buy my lady this ring. That's what a man does." The big-haired blonde clutching the football fan's arm preened.

Steve gritted his teeth. "I'll buy the ring." He bit out the words. Feeling more than seeing the still-condemning expressions on the faces of his fellow customers, he bared his teeth and added, "Rings."

"But that's just silly." She patted his arm. His sore arm. "I told you when you agreed to this marriage thing, I'd take care of the costs. A deal's a deal."

She turned to the now wide-eyed clerk. "Show us what you have, please."

"Di, di, did you have a price range in mind?" The bemused fellow stammered out his question as though he was having trouble catching his breath.

Steve was feeling a bit strangled, himself. Or was that just an urge to strangle someone else? A certain redhead with no sense of propriety?

"Do you have any clearance stuff?" Her face lit up. "Or, I know, something that somebody else returned. You know, they broke up or something? Have anything marked down?"

He moaned.

The Bronco's fan snorted.

A suspicious gleam had crept into the clerk's eyes. "Wait a minute. Is this *Spy TV*, or *Candid Camera* or something?" He swiveled his head back and forth. "Am I on tape?"

A collective "ahhh" spread through the crowd at what appeared to be the only explanation for the bride's astonishing disclosures.

Okay, he'd had enough. "Just show us some rings!" He barked at the clerk in a tone louder than any used by the most frightened of his patients. But it worked. The darting glances he cast around the room suggested the clerk still believed a camera was recording this bizarre transaction, but in seconds a tray of rings appeared before their eyes.

Nina quickly picked out the least expensive set available, serviceable gold bands with no embellishments.

"Um, are they returnable?" She cast a twinkling glance sideways at him before turning to the salesman again. "I have a feeling this thing might last only a week or so."

The clerk's eyes bugged out for a moment, but then, his expression wooden, he said only, "We have a thirty day return policy."

"Perfect!"

Steve eyed the thin, plain bands. "I don't like them."

"Don't be silly. They're just right. And the price is much better than I expected." She pulled out her checkbook, but Steve snatched it from her fingers and slid it back into her purse.

"No, not these. And you are not paying."

"But—"

Interrupting her, he whispered in a crisp monotone, "A surgeon would give his bride something a little more ostentatious."

A brief shrug dismissed that concern. "Maybe so, but you can be a cheap surgeon." When he did not laugh, she added, "Steve, they cost too—"

"I said, I'm buying." As if cost were a concern to him. In fact, right now he could not remember a time he had ever been glad for the very high limit on his American Express Card. He could buy out the store if he wanted, and right now, he wanted.

But question marks danced in her eyes, and he didn't have answers. So he made one up. "I'm not having a bunch of people on a damned boat thinking I'm a cheapskate." There. That sounded good. If the woman was going to pose as his wife, she'd damn well look the part. Sandra had sported a rock the size of Gibraltar, after all.

"But it's not very likely you'll ever see those people again. Why should you care?"

He didn't know the answer to that question, either, so instead of answering he asked one of his own. "What about your grandmother? Won't she be indignant if you don't have an expensive engagement ring?"

"Grams won't give the cost of the ring a thought. Besides, we eloped. A whirlwind romance. No time for a fancy ring." She pulled him toward the cash register. "Let's just get these and get to the airport."

Turning her smile to the clerk again, she said, "Don't bother with a bag. We'll just put 'em on." Sliding the smaller ring onto her left hand, she handed him the other. "We might as well get used to the feel, don't you think?"

"No."

But his opinion was ignored. "Anything you say, Miss." The salesclerk had obviously decided he was going to uphold the dignity of the store, no matter how ridiculous the customers were. White teeth showing, he added gamely, "Let me just total this sale up."

She started to follow the clerk to the sales counter, but Steve reached out for her arm and held her back. She was going to wear his rings, regardless of what she thought about the matter.

His rings. He liked the sound of that. Liked the thought of her wearing his brand.

"Honey." Loud enough that heads turned toward them again. "I want to get a nicer set. And an engagement ring." Even as he spoke the words, he wondered whether he'd be able to find a good shrink in Denver to examine his head. Still, he added, "I insist." He folded his arms in front of his chest, making it clear he would not go another step until he got his way.

Wordlessly, she came back to the display case. Steve pointed out the set he wanted her to have. Wanted her to wear. The engagement ring had a deceptively small but perfectly cut diamond, with two emeralds, one on each side. The engraved scrollwork on the wedding band matched both the engagement ring and the groom's ring. Overall, the effect was not nearly as flashy as the goose egg Sandra had insisted upon, but much more elegant.

The rings fit perfectly. The emeralds matched her eyes. The clerk's jaw dropped at the name on the credit card, but he said nothing more as he totaled the sale and handed over the receipt. No doubt he was too busy planning how to spend his astronomical commission check.

Steve hadn't ever been one for believing in fate, but at that moment, he wondered whether his own was sealed.

Back in the cab, Nina studied the rings. They felt strange on her hand.

Normally, she never wore rings. Earrings, necklaces, bracelets—she had dozens of each. She loved beads of every color, and prided herself on her collection of imaginative jewelry from around the world.

But no rings. Something about those unbroken circles had always suggested commitment to her.

Permanence. Finality. She knew where that sort of thing led. A dead end. So she steered clear of rings.

But none of those nasty feelings emanated from these rings. No, they felt warm. Steadying.

They just looked so *right*. Like they'd been made just for her. Anyone looking at that engagement ring would definitely believe a man who loved her picked it out. A man who knew her better than anyone.

She smiled at Steve. Odd, but it did feel like she'd known him forever. Which was good, because husbands and wives know everything about each other.

"Omigosh!" She sat bolt upright. Turning her head, she gaped at Steve. "Husbands and wives know everything about each other!"

Steve returned her stare, a wary look in his eyes. "Okaaay," he drawled. Raising his brows, he added, "And . . . ?"

"And?" She nearly shrieked. "And I don't know your shoe size. I don't know how you take your coffee. I don't know your mother's maiden name." She fluttered her hands in front of herself. "I know *nothing* about you."

She pulled out her PDA. After a brief chew on the end of the stylus, she began jotting down questions. When they arrived at the airport, she thrust it into Steve's face.

"Here. You need to answer these questions so I can memorize them. Let's check the bags curbside so we can get started."

They hurried as best they could through the ticket and security lines. When they were finally on the way to the trains that traveled to the concourse, he took the PDA from her and began to read.

"Well, have you finished yet?" she asked?

"Finished? What's to finish?" He read her list out loud. "Aftershave? Favorite TV shows? What is this?"

"If we are going to convince Grams we're married, we have to know about each other."

"C'mon, this is nuts. You think your grandmother is going to grill us? Give us a pop quiz? About things like this?" He continued to read her notes. "Favorite color? Favorite food? Favorite poem?"

He gave her that look she got a bit too often. The one suggesting he thought she ought to be committed.

"A wife would know her husband's favorite poem." She winced at the defensive note in her voice. "Wouldn't she?"

"Maybe. If her husband had one. Trust me, your

husband doesn't." He shook his head. "And even if I did, I don't think Granny would ask what it is."

"Grams, not Granny. See, that is something you should know." She took a deep breath. "We've got to make it look like we've been living together for months."

They reached the platform of the trains that led to the concourse. Luckily, a train was just pulling in and they hustled on.

She glanced at his chiseled profile. How could she convince anyone this stranger was her husband? His tailored look made her more freewheeling style seem so out of place. Frankly, he was a bit out of her league. He continued his review of her hastily scribbled list, chuckling. Even if it was directed at her, she liked the sound of his deep rich laugh. Somehow it didn't really feel like he laughed at her, the way it did with so many other men she'd known. Instead, he seemed to include her in the amusement.

"Lord, this sounds like the Newlywed Game." A sound somewhere between a snort and a guffaw echoed off the train's interior. "Boxers or briefs! Why d'ya want to know that?"

Several heads swiveled in their direction. Nina sank onto the seat at the end of the car, feeling a hot blush steal over her.

"Well, a wife would know," she muttered.

He glanced down at her. "Yeah. I guess a wife would know that one." His voice drawled over her slowly, almost as slowly as the gaze that caressed her body.

"Does that mean I get to find out what you're wearing under that lacy blouse?"

Unbidden, the image of the two of them engaged in a very private fashion show popped into her head. She swallowed hard. The heat of her blush intensified.

"Just go on to the next one, will you?" She turned to look out the window at the flashing mobiles that decorated the walls of the train tunnel. Yet despite her prim reply, she couldn't resist stealing a sidelong glance at the jeans that tightly encased Steve's muscular thighs.

Briefs? She couldn't tell.

"Boxers." The low whisper sent a shiver through her.

Her gaze lifted to his face. A gray eye winked. Turning her view back to the windows, she felt certain her cheeks now matched her hair.

"Just, just write your answers down, okay?"

Steve could not tear his eyes from the delicate rose that tinted Nina's cheeks. Somewhere in the recesses of his mind, he heard his mother's voice saying that redheads should never wear pink but Mother obviously did not know best. *This* redhead was very pretty in pink.

Pretty, hell! She was gorgeous.

Maybe he wouldn't regret this trip, after all. Shoot, he could have a good time just watching the parade of emotions cross her lovely face. Spending a week with her could definitely yield some nice benefits. Aside from missing the social whirlwind and humiliation his ex-wife intended to impose on him.

A computerized tinkling signaled their arrival at the C concourse. Nina jumped up.

"This one is us." Her cheeks still infused with color, she seemed to be having trouble meeting his eyes. He let her rush ahead of him. He rather liked the view of the gentle sway of her hips as she led him to their gate. Despite her shy looks just now, she moved confidently, her long legs striding with practiced ease across the marble floors to their gate.

Her skin looked as soft and smooth as satin. Unbidden, the image of Nina in a French-cut bikini filled his mind. No doubt the cruise would have some stop over time at a tropical port. With her creamy skin, she'd need lots of sunblock stroked on. And he knew just the man for that job.

The warmth of that tropical sun must be pretty strong because he could feel it already. He loosened his collar.

A voice over the loudspeaker interrupted his reverie. "Air Alaska Flight 304 to Anchorage is now ready for boarding. Passengers with small children—"

"Air Alaska?" His incredulous question was loud enough to drown out the remainder of the gate attendant's spiel, and again heads turned. Ignoring the onlookers, he bored his gaze into the back of the tousled red curls. He did not lower his voice as he added, "Anchorage?"

Innocent green eyes turned to him with a questioning look. "What's wrong?"

Chapter Three

"What's wrong?" he echoed. "Our plane is going to Anchorage! That's what's wrong!"

"Well, duh!" Her head tilted to the side as she stared back at him. "Of course, the plane is going to Anchorage. We set sail from Seward. Oh, did you think we were going on the Northbound cruise? Those leave from Vancouver."

At her words, his happy fantasies of sun drenched beaches, and water drenched bikinis dissolved. Immediately, his mind filled the void with an image of Nina standing on an iceberg, wrapped in a bulky fur parka. So much for smoothing sunblock over her silky skin. How could he do that if he had mittens on?

"An Alaskan cruise? But you said . . ." His voice trailed off. No, actually, when he thought back on it, she hadn't said anything about tropical locales. When he'd heard the word "cruise," he'd just assumed she meant a cruise in the tropics. The Bahamas, Jamaica, Cancun. Or maybe the Mexican Riviera. Alaska had simply never occurred to him.

Damn!

He didn't want to go to Alaska. He didn't mind the cold. Heck, he'd spent too much time in the hockey rinks to be bothered by it, but he hated snow. Even though it was late spring, there was bound to be some snow in Alaska. He'd only moved back to Denver after remembering the three hundred days of sunshine every year. Plenty of snow in the mountains to the west, but relatively little down on the plains in Denver.

Spending time with this lady might be worth a lot of sacrifices, but snow? Not to mention the immunizations he had to get.

Immunizations? This time the heat under his collar wasn't caused by thoughts of lying on a beach with her.

Through his teeth, he asked, "If we are going to Alaska, part of the good old U.S. of A., why did I have to get those damn shots?"

"The shots?" She shrugged. "You just have to get them when you go on a cruise."

"That's ridiculous. Why?"

"How should I know why? You just do. I know because when I took a cruise to South America, I had to get them."

He counted to ten. By the time he finished counting, a burning red haze tinted everything he looked at. He counted to twenty this time, and took a deep breath, preparing a speech designed to wilt her curls.

But before he said a word, a soft, silky touch stroked

his wrist. He felt a tingle run up his arm and spread out to the rest of him.

"Does it *still* hurt?"

He looked down into her concerned face, and forgot the flaming insults he'd intended to hurl at her.

Hurt? He wouldn't describe it as hurting, exactly. More of a quivering, jolting sort of sensation where her fingers still connected with his skin. No, it didn't hurt.

"Your arm?" Her gaze dropped to the shoulder where he'd received most of the shots. "It doesn't hurt anymore?"

He shook his head.

"And your," she started to look around at his rear, but stopped herself with a blush, "the place you got the other shot?"

Anger forgotten in the face of her genuine concern, he smiled. "No, the other place doesn't hurt either." He motioned her to precede him onto the plane.

He didn't have the heart to point out the lack of necessity for the immunizations. On the bright side, he didn't have to worry about picking up any of those rare arctic diseases. Like malaria or typhoid.

She'd meant well, after all.

I meant well. Nina continued to repeat the phrase that had been her mantra since they'd arrived at the ship. *I never meant to create this tissue of lies.* All she had wanted was to keep Grams happy and well.

And Grams did look well. Her snowy hair was coifed in a practical but elegant style. The brightness of the green eyes gleaming out from the wrinkled but still beautiful face belied her seventy plus years. Spry in her bright yellow cropped pants and espadrilles, Grams looked like she just walked off the cover of *Modern Maturity*.

She had also looked a bit surprised when Nina introduced Steve to her, but then again, his movie star good looks were a bit stunning. Even Ana, who as a sports photographer hobnobbed with hunky guys all the time, had been a bit startled at the sight of him.

"Way to go, Sis," she'd whispered as she snapped a few shots of them. "You know, he looks kind of familiar . . ."

And there had been that awkward moment when Steve had blurted out, "You're Rebecca Anderson," to Grams. Somehow, she must have forgotten to tell him just who Grams was. She'd mentioned her grandmother was an artist, but hadn't thought to say how well known her funky paintings of cows in improbable sports attire and situations had become, what with the greeting card line and calendars and everything. Fortunately, Steve had managed to smooth that over by saying he'd expected a much older woman. Ana had rolled her eyes a bit, but their grandmother had been pleased enough. In fact, she'd gotten comfortable with her supposed grandson-in-law a bit too quickly, and was now making big plans.

"What's the big idea of hogging my granddaughter all to yourself?" After wrapping her arms around as much of his broad shoulders as she could reach, Grams lowered her white brows with mock severity. "Now you two are just going to have to find time to come visit me in Murraysville. I know Idaho isn't nearly as exciting as Denver, but we have some sights, you know."

Latching onto Steve's arm, she hauled him up the gangplank, leaving Nina to trail behind with Ana. Her sister had spent a week with Grams in their home town before the two traveled together to Anchorage, and wanted to share the gossip about their old high school friends. In between her sister's enthusiastic updates, Nina caught snatches of Grams' conversation.

"So Millie Wiggs married John . . ."

". . . Christmas is a lovely time . . ."

". . . believe it, Honey Williams is pregnant again. This is their . . ."

". . . sleigh rides, caroling, . . ."

"Brent Patterson is back in town . . ."

"Thanksgiving would be even better . . ."

"Grams!" Nina finally found her voice as they halted outside the cabin her grandmother and sister would share. "Don't you go badgering Steve about his schedule. He has to put in a lot of hours in the operating room." She gave a titter that sounded unconvincing even to her ears. "You know I told you what a time I had convincing him to take time off for this cruise. Let's not spoil it with demands for more."

"Yes, well, I'm glad he's a good provider, but family counts a lot too." She narrowed her eyes at him. "Right, Steve?"

"Right, Mrs., uh, Ma'am."

"No, don't you Ma'am me, you rapscallion. I'm on to you." A faint look of alarm crossed his face, while

Nina drew in a long breath and held it. "My granddaughter has already told me how you refer to me as Grams, so you can just do it straight to my face."

Nina released the air from her lungs while Steve pasted a sick grin to his face. "Sure, Ma'—, I mean, Grams."

A wizened head shook. "You don't look like any doctor I ever had." A wrinkled nose sniffed. "But still, a doctor in the family is a good thing. Now, Stevie, I have this ache in my side sometimes, right here." She pressed his hand against her waist.

Nina tried to intervene. "There's a ship doctor, Grams, if you're feeling ill. Are you feeling seasick?"

"Of course I'm not feeling seasick. I just got on this boat. Besides, we're still in port. And I don't want a ship doctor. What's wrong with Stevie, here?"

"I'm sorry, Grams, but I'm not an internist." Steve's voice was a bit strained as he pulled his hand back, but Nina was impressed at his quick thinking.

"Right, right. He's a surgeon."

"What kind?" Ana had been silently watching this interchange until now, taking a few pictures with the camera she always kept close at hand. Nina had been thinking how nice it was to see her sister. But now she rather wished her sister had stayed in New York where she belonged.

"You didn't tell them what kind of surgeon I am, darling?" Her "husband" turned his head toward her. His pewter eyes brimmed with laughter.

She almost forgot the abyss looming before her in

her indignation at his enjoyment of this first obstacle in their path. But *had* she said what kind of surgeon her phantom husband was? She couldn't remember.

"Oh, I'm sure I did." She looked from Grams to Ana and back at Grams again. Two pairs of green eyes, so like her own, stared back at her. "You remember. Don't you?"

Two heads shook slightly.

"Oh. Well, he's a, a, a plastic surgeon!"

Those green eyes shifted their focus to Steve. A soft "wow" escaped her sister's lips. Grams frowned.

Feeling more was needed, Nina added, "He's had a lot of big stars. Cher, even! That's, that's why he's so busy. Lots of stars . . ." Her voice trailed off.

"Plastic surgeon. That's mighty impressive, young man." A hint of uncertainty laced the aged voice. "I guess."

"Yeah, it is, isn't it?" Steve glowered at Nina. "All those celebrities and all."

"Humph. I guess modesty isn't your long suit."

"Well, Grams, it is pretty cool. Just think, my very own husband," she slipped her hand around his waist, "is on a first name basis with all kinds of movie stars."

"Like Cher?" A cackle escaped her grandmother.

"Hey, Cher won an Oscar!" Nina tried to look indignant. She hoped a nice discussion of the merits of crossing lines of talent could take the attention off her supposed marriage. "She's not like other singers who use their fame to get into the movies."

It was not to be.

"Since when do movie stars go to Denver for plastic surgery?" Ana frowned as she posed the question.

Nina couldn't believe the skepticism in her sweet little sister's voice. Life in the big city had obviously been a bad influence on her. She glanced at Steve, looking for help. All she got was a grim smile in return.

"Um, well, yeah, they don't want everyone in Hollywood to know, so they come to Denver to sort of hide out." Had that sounded as lame to her family as it had to her? She gave a nervous giggle.

Grams stared intently at Nina for a moment and then turned to her other granddaughter. "Come on, Ana. Let's leave these love birds and get settled in."

Love birds? Oh, lordy, they'd forgotten to act like a married couple. Except for her single touch, the way she and Steve had been standing so stiffly, anyone would think they were total strangers. Not at all like the happily married couple she wanted Grams to believe.

She immediately went all out to remedy the impression. "Yes, we're anxious to find our cabin too. Aren't we, *Honey?* I think we're just a little down the passage here. Honey." Nina put her arm around Steve's waist again and pasted a grin on her face. Responding to the pressure of her fingers, Steve laid his arm across her shoulders. A smile was pinned to his face, as well.

Ana and Grams exchanged glances, but merely nodded as they proceeded through their own cabin door.

As soon as Ana and Grams were inside their cabin with the door shut, Steve turned on his "wife." "A plastic surgeon? My god, are you nuts? Couldn't you have said orthopedic surgeon or something? Did it have to be so, so shallow?" Plastic surgeon to the stars? Sheesh.

"No, I am not nuts." Green fire flashed at him from beneath long auburn eyelashes. "Think about it. Grams won't be asking you to perform any liposuction for her."

He raised one finger to argue the point, but stopped. Okay, so that made sense. "You have a point there," he conceded with reluctance. He'd thought it funny at first when Grams had asked for a diagnosis, but he knew enough about human medicine to know the wrong advice could be pretty serious. Especially for an elderly woman. "I guess plastic surgery was a smart choice, after all."

The compliment was mild, offhand even, but her reaction suggested a lottery jackpot win. The now familiar oomph in his gut hit him again when she turned that brilliant smile on him. Her broad grin brightened even the far corners of the corridor leading to their cabin.

Looking at the key in his hand, he found their door. He unlocked it, and pushed it open to allow her to precede him. Her delicate floral scent wafted under his nose as she brushed lightly past him. With difficulty, he resisted a sudden impulse to lean down and breathe in more fully. Instead, he glanced around.

The room was small. Smaller than the typical hotel room. Opposite the door, twin beds were pushed against each wall. Their luggage had already been delivered, and was stacked neatly at the foot of one of the beds. A small bureau stood between the beds, and a tiny porthole peeped out above the bureau.

Just inside the door sat another dresser, topped with a long wall mirror that extended along so it also topped a desk and chair. To the left, he could see the open bathroom door revealing a serviceable shower stall. Another door probably hid a closet.

The accommodations were what you would expect on a ship where the idea was to offer every conceivable sort of entertainment, all taking place outside the room. Not at all shabby, but not exactly luxurious either.

But the quarters were definitely cramped. The thought cheered him up a bit. He would be spending at least eight hours every night for the next six nights in a room alone with Nina. With those beds less than three feet apart, he had a feeling pretending to be "plastic surgeon to the stars" was a small price to pay.

She stood in the middle of the room and flung her arms out. "Well, here we are. I guess we might as well unpack while we wait for them to shove off." She pulled her suitcase up onto one of the beds and unzipped it.

"Another sensible suggestion." This earned him another happy smile.

He picked up his bag and set it on the bed she had not claimed. He pulled out his shirts and slacks and hung them in the small closet, frowning a bit at the wrinkles. He'd have to have them pressed. The rest of his clothes fit snugly into a drawer. He set his toiletry bag next to the sink. Finished in less than five minutes, he had plenty of time to observe the more drawn out event that was Nina unpacking. He sat on his bed to watch.

She had opened her bag and pulled out what appeared to be a huge bundle of cloth. But there seemed to be some method to her madness as she peeled layer after layer from the bundle and stowed each item neatly in the closet.

"I've never seen anyone pack like that." Nothing was folded exactly, but when she pulled a blouse off the stack, he could see it was completely crease free. "How do you keep them from getting all wrinkled?"

"I do a lot of traveling, you know. There are definitely some tricks to painless packing."

He nodded. A travel writer would pack and unpack a lot.

She cocked her head. "You know, that might make a good title for an article." Abandoning her unpacking, she pulled out her PDA. She made a note with the stylus and then went back to her task.

The seriousness with which she approached her work impressed him. She had the same dedication to her field that his mother had shown to hers. Caring about doing a job well was not something that ever seemed that important among the crowd that surrounded his father's family.

Returning to her suitcase, Nina continued. "I've learned how to pack things properly over the years." She shook out one of her gauzy skirts before attaching it to a hanger. "The secret is to roll your clothes, not fold them."

Her efficiency and skill fascinated him. She seemed so flighty and airheaded at times, yet somehow she had the knack of always seeming to fit her surroundings perfectly.

He envied her that ability. He had never had it. He'd always felt out of place, whether in his father's mansion or his mother's more modest house.

He continued to stare as she turned back to her task. The bundle shrunk item by item until all articles of her colorful and comfortable looking clothing had vanished into the closet.

She pulled a smaller collection from her bag. These were not rolled together in the same way as the other pieces of clothing. As she pulled a lacy bra free of the pile, his heartbeat quickened. His cheeks warmed a bit, but he could not look away.

She had the most feminine underthings he'd ever seen.

Not titillating. His ex-wife had gone for the sleaziest of Victoria's Secret's offerings, or maybe Frederick's of Hollywood was the source. But Nina obviously favored the sweet lines of lingerie.

Nina's underclothes weren't sexy. At least, not overtly.

But they made his blood race. Pastel panties with flimsy matching brassieres. A lacy slip in a modest beige. Nothing in its color or design suggested her underwear was intended to provoke passion in the male breast.

Yet, as she shook out each item before placing it in the drawer, he felt his blood pressure rise. In his mind's eye, he could see each article of clothing against her creamy gold skin.

The cabin suddenly seemed too close, too confining.

The beds, which were really smaller than the average

twin beds, suddenly seemed overwhelming in their suggestiveness.

"Right!" He stood suddenly, sitting having become a painful exercise. Rubbing his hands together, his gaze darted around the cabin, looking for any distraction from the direction his thoughts had taken. He didn't think he'd get too far if he made a move before the ship had even set sail.

He started toward the door. "I think I'm going to go back up on deck!"

"Oh, okay. Let me just put my make-up bag in the bathroom, and I'll join you."

"Fine, fine." He nodded sharply, trying not to let his eyes stray to a wisp of pale blue lace that peeked out of the drawer she had just closed.

She pulled a small colorful bag from the suitcase and closed the suitcase, returning it to its former place on the floor. Holding her make-up case, she started toward the bathroom, but stopped as he blocked her way.

"Excuse me."

He backed against the desk chair, but the small passage required her to brush against him as she passed. He failed to stifle the groan that erupted as her hip slipped along his thigh.

She stopped at the sound. "Oh, I'm sorry! Did I step on your foot?" Question marks formed in the wide gaze she turned to him. She wet her lips.

The sight of her pink tongue nearly undid him. Mutely, he shook his head. The urge to take her into his arms nearly overwhelmed him.

She leaned toward him, her lips pursing slightly.

A sudden rapping sound at their door caused her to jump away, confusion flowing swiftly across her face.

"Yoo hoo! Nina? Steve?" Grams' cheerful voice filled the room. "The ship's about to leave port. Do you want to come up on deck to wave and throw streamers like they do on television?"

Grateful for the interruption, Steve practically lunged at the door to open it. "Hey, Grams!" He waved his hand toward the interior of the cabin. "C'mon in."

She beamed back at him as she walked in, but her face fell as she took in the Spartan nature of the stateroom. "But your room is just like Ana's and mine."

Nina cocked her head at her grandmother. "Well, yeah, Grams, what did you expect?"

The older woman tsked as she looked around the small room. "But honey, you told me this cruise was going to be like the honeymoon you and Steve never took. I thought you'd have one of the special rooms." Chagrin filled her voice as she cast a disappointed look Steve's way. "You don't even have a double bed."

"We prefer twin beds," Steve said immediately.

"The suites were all filled," Nina said at the same time.

Her lips twitched slightly as Grams looked from one to the other, one slim gray eyebrow raised. "So which is it?"

He stared at his "wife," not wanting to jump on her words again. But she seemed at a loss, raising her eyebrows back at him with a pleading expression.

Grams crossed her arms and tapped a foot, looking

as formidable as a five-foot-two-inch woman in her seventies could look. "Well?"

An entirely illogical sense of guilt at failing to measure up in the indulgent husband department swept over him. So if Nina was going to leave the explanation to him, it was damn well going to make him look good.

"Well, Grams, it's like this." He leaned against the desk and crossed his own arms. "You know how Nina has this 'Solitary Traveler' thing going, so she has really been reluctant to take me along on any of her trips. And the only way I could get her to agree to let me come along on this one was if I agreed to stay in one of these cabins with the single beds. That way, she'd still be sure to have the same experiences of someone traveling alone."

Green eyes, only slightly faded with age, narrowed slightly, measuring him. A faint smile crossed her lips as she gave the smallest of nods, and then a wink.

A wink? What the hey?

But then she turned away from him with a briskness that belied her age. "Nina! You said Steve couldn't travel with you because of his schedule. Do you mean to tell me you've been untruthful to me?"

"Tsk, tsk. Shame on you, Nina." He put his best saintly expression on his face, even as he stored away his thoughts about what Grams was thinking. "You haven't been telling whoppers to your grandmother, have you?"

Green sparks flashed at him as Nina glared his way. Then she lifted her chin before replying. "Grams, I swear to you, Steve has not been available to travel with me until now. In fact, he agreed to go on this cruise *for certain* only yesterday." Peering over her grandmother's shoulder, she challenged him to deny that simple truth.

He snorted, but gave a slight bow of his head to acknowledge her triumph. When he said nothing more, she continued, "By the time I knew for sure he was coming with me, it was too late for a suite."

"But you told me a month ago he was coming on this cruise. 'A belated honeymoon' were your exact words."

For a moment, the redhead was stymied. But she recovered quickly. "Positive thinking, Grams. You always told me to use positive thinking." She waved her hand in his direction. "You see—it worked."

"Hmmph. Well, I think you could have thought positively enough for a fancy room for your first trip together." But the cat's eyes twinkled at Steve as she groused out her complaint.

"It's not a bad room, Grams. You said yourself that you and Ana have one just like it."

"Your sister and I aren't on a honeymoon. But what can't be mended must be endured." A thoughtful expression crossed her face. "Although I wonder if it can't be mended."

"What do you mean, Grams?" The suspicion in her voice suggested Grams was a lady who bore watching.

"Oh, nothing, dear." The gray head shook. "I am just disappointed. I hoped this trip would be special for the two of you." There was just enough reproach in the glance she cast him to cause him another jolt of irrational remorse.

Oh, this lady was good. Very good. If he really were married to her granddaughter, he'd be racking his brain trying to figure out how to fix the accommodations.

In fact, now that he thought about it, there was no reason why he couldn't check into an upgrade. That would definitely score points with Grams, and he had a hunch that pleasing Grams would please his faux bride.

Not that she seemed too concerned about her grandmother's disappointment in the room. "Trust me, once you and Ana see all the great things you can do on the cruise, you won't worry about the room. What do you think we'd do in the cabin anyway? Trust me, the fun stuff is definitely in other parts of the ship."

He covered his eyes with one hand in resignation. Great. Just, great. If he were truly a recent bridegroom, he'd certainly be feeling a bit chagrined at what was a damning condemnation of his amorous skills. As it was, he couldn't prevent the heat rising in his neck. What must this sweet old woman be thinking of him?

But Grams merely laughed heartily, and gave her granddaughter a hug. "Oh, honey. You are so sweet." The older woman straightened, and added with an arch look his way, "There's no need to pretend."

He exchanged a glance with Nina, who seemed struck mute. "There's not?" he prompted.

"Of course not. I do know what husbands and wives do." She patted her granddaughter's cheek. "Where do you think your mother came from, silly?"

"Oh." An audible sigh of relief escaped Nina. Then, her eyes grew wide. "Oh! I didn't . . . that is, we have fun, lots of fun . . . I mean . . ." Pink suffused her face as she trailed off. She cast him a look of entreaty.

An evil sense of getting his own back caused him to respond, "Absolutely, lots of fun. I hope the people in the cabins on either side don't mind a bit of noise, because Nina can be a bit loud."

Those jade eyes widened in horror as the pink turned to a bright tomato red.

But Grams merely chortled and gifted them both with an affectionate smile. "Oh, you are a wicked one. But trust me, I know. There's no better way to keep a marriage happy and make it last."

With those sage words, she marched out of the room, but not before sending another knowing look his way. After giving him a scolding glare that promised retribution later, Nina trailed after her.

He stayed behind a moment. Unless he missed his guess, Grams was on to the redhead's little scam. But for some reason, she was playing along. But why would she play along? And why did she keep winking at him?

He had a feeling it would be a most interesting week.

Chapter Four

Even though the ship left port at nine o'clock at night, the Alaskan sun was far from setting and there was plenty of light for the Mardi Gras atmosphere of a bon voyage party. Music played, streamers swirled through the air, and the passengers crowded the rails to wave at friends, family, and strangers standing ashore. This was Nina's fourth cruise, but she still took pleasure in the excitement of the cheering and laughing around her.

Even more, she reveled in the pure enjoyment writ across the faces of the two people she loved most in the world, her grandmother and her sister. Snow-covered mountains and bright blue glaciers filled the eyes as the ship began its travel out to sea. Her years based in Denver had made jagged peaks tipped with white the normal backdrop for her life, but the sheer height and stark beauty of the summits could not fail to impress the flatlanders. Even Steve, who was doing her such a favor, looked like he was enjoying himself.

All was well with the world.

But the excitement of the shove-off ended all too quickly.

"Well, now, I guess the four of us can settle down and have a nice talk now." A look of steely determination in Grams' eyes told Nina there would be no putting off this conversation.

Oh well, she'd always been good at pop quizzes. And after all, this is what she and Steve had studied up for on the plane. On the other hand, she'd never been too good at fibbing. When she was a kid, making up stories had always made her feel a bit feverish. She learned the truth was usually easier.

But Grams had been so happy about her 'marriage,' she had to get through this.

"I'm really anxious for the two of you to get to know Steve as well as I do." She gestured toward the Lido Grill on the Promenade deck. "Let's sit over here. We can still see the scenery this way."

Pretending a nonchalance she was far from feeling, she led the way to an empty corner next to a huge window. Was there anything she and Steve hadn't covered? She never had found out his favorite poem. Did he say he didn't have one? As she settled into her chair, she fanned herself with her hand. It was surprisingly warm so far north.

Turning her attention to her companions, she waited

for the barrage of questions her family was sure to throw at Steve and her.

Grams buttoned the cardigan of her sweater set. "Will a waiter come and take an order for drinks or do we need to go over to that bar?"

"Oh, uh, yeah, there's a waiter, he'll be over here soon, I'm sure." Was that a shiver she saw in her grandmother? "Are you feeling okay, Grams?"

"Oh, just fine, dear. It's just a tad cool in here."

Her grandmother looked as healthy as Nina had ever seen her, but how could she be chilly in this sweltering heat?

"Yes, the breeze is pretty strong." Ana rubbed her arms. Her short-sleeved top exposed goose flesh from above her elbow to her wrists.

Steve's face showed none of the anxiety threatening to overwhelm Nina. He stopped in the middle of unrolling his white cotton shirt sleeves to cover his own arms. "If you ladies are feeling a mite cool, why don't we all just move below deck and get out of the wind?"

"Oh, no!" Both chilled ladies immediately refused this offer. "The view is so nice. I wouldn't want to miss it," Grams added.

"But maybe you girls should be wearing more than those short sleeves."

"I do think I'll go down and grab a sweater. Sis, do you want a wrap?"

Nina shook her head mutely. A sweater? Her sister had to be kidding.

"Okay. I'll be right back. Order me a hot chocolate."

Hot chocolate? When it was hot as blazes! She dabbed with a napkin at a bit of perspiration on her upper lip and stared with an open mouth at her sister's retreating form.

"Oh, yes. Warm drinks are just what we need." Grams smiled happily as the waiter arrived. She ordered tea for herself, hot chocolate for Ana, and looked expectantly at Nina and Steve.

"I'll have coffee black. And she'll," Steve nodded at Nina, "have a double tall, half no-fat, mocha latte, with chocolate sprinkles."

Nina blinked at his recitation of her favorite coffee drink. That hadn't been on the list she'd insisted he study. That could only mean he'd remembered what she ordered in the coffeehouse where she'd told him about the cruise. Touched by such solicitude, she reached out to pat his hand, only to feel a jolting spark as she made contact with his skin.

From the way he'd straightened in his chair, it was clear he'd felt it too. Their gazes met, and they laughed at the same moment.

"Static electricity." She shrugged.

"Yeah. But seems a bit odd, considering it's so humid," he murmured back.

She glanced a bit uncertainly at him, but his attention was focused on Grams. Turning to look at her grand-mother, Nina felt a lightening in her heart. Judging by the smug smile on Grams' face, they were off to a good start in convincing her of their happy marriage. She leaned back in her chair, realizing for the first time how stiffly she had been holding herself.

"Steve, my granddaughter really hasn't told me much about your background. Tell me about yourself."

Nina sat bolt upright again. What had she told her grandmother? Anything that Steve should know? She couldn't remember.

After the briefest of questioning glances in her direction, Steve turned back to the older woman and shrugged. "I don't rightly know what there is to tell, Ma'am. I was born in Colorado, but after my parents divorced, I mostly grew up in Texas. I spent summers with my Dad in Colorado."

"And what made you decide to be a doctor? Was your father a doctor too?

"No, no. He was something of an early pioneer in electronics and computers."

Nina's jaw dropped. Computers? He was a Tabor whose father worked in computers. Was he one of *those* Tabors, after all? That family was worth millions. He couldn't—

With a start, she noticed her grandmother viewing her. She dropped her eyes and tried to concentrate on what her "husband" was saying.

"I guess I spent so much time helping my mother out it just seemed natural enough for me to carry on the same line of work when I grew up."

A short silence greeted those words. Pale lips pursed as Grams mulled over his words.

"Heh, heh. I told you he had a great sense of humor, didn't I? Same line of work. Ha, ha." Raising her hand to shield her face from her grandmother's view, she rolled her eyes at him.

Steve started as he realized his mistake and then emitted a short uncomfortable laugh of his own. Trying to recover, he offered, "Well, you know, in the ranch-land of Texas, our animals are pretty much members of the family. People doctoring didn't seem like much of a stretch."

"I don't imagine that plastic surgery seems very close to your mother's field, though."

"Er, no, but my mother doesn't mind. She just wants me to be happy."

That non sequitur seemed an appropriate end to the issue of his profession. Grams' next question took a different tack. "So why'd you end up back in Denver instead of Dallas?"

"I moved there because Nina was there?" The question in Steve's voice seemed obvious to Nina, but went unnoticed by her grandmother.

"Well, that's sweet. But I thought Nina told me you did your residency at a Denver hospital." Grams smiled at Nina. "Isn't that what you told me, dear?"

She felt like a deer trapped in headlights as two gazes bored into her. "Did I say that?"

But her knight in shining armor swept in to save her. "No, you must have misunderstood, Grams. It was my undergraduate work that I did in Denver. At the University of Denver. I played hockey."

"Hockey?" Grams brightened. "So you skate too. That's something you have in common."

Seeing confusion slipping into Steve's expression, Nina jumped in. "Oh, yes. We love to skate together. We go to the DU rink all the time." Under the table, she reached for Steve's leg and squeezed. His brows rose, but he backed her up.

"Yeah. They built a new one since I was in school. Very nice."

"Wonderful!" Grams smiled as she folded her hands beneath her chin. "I'm so glad you have a nice healthy hobby. I worry that the two of you work too hard."

Nina sighed with a mixture of relief and contentment. So far, so good. And, wow—this guy was good, very good. She grinned happily at the wisdom of her choice. He was going to breeze through this inquisition without a hitch.

Her sister returned to the table just as their drinks arrived. For a few moments, they all sipped in happy silence, watching the green and white land recede as the ship headed out to sea. Seagulls gave their eerie calls as they flew overhead, and the occasional fish jumped in a wide arc above the water.

Nina wiped the last bit of whipped cream from her lips and beamed at her companions. "So, what activities do you want to do this week?"

"I intend to take lots of photos. These cliffs will make a nice change from jocks." Ana turned her serene smile to Steve. "But otherwise, you have to tell us what things are the most fun. There are so many to choose from I don't know where to begin. What do you like to do on a cruise?"

"I've never been on a cruise before, Ma'am, so I'm as new at it as you are."

His wide smile dimmed as his words were met with an upraised brow. Nina squirmed in her seat again, all assurance lost. Her heart sank to levels rivaling the depth of the channel through which the ship passed. How could she have forgotten to tell him of his proposal? It was so romantic too—on a cruise of the Greek Isles.

"You mean, never on a big cruise ship like this?" Ana asked. He wasn't sure if Ana was trying to make sense of the inconsistency of his words with the information obviously given by her sister, or if she was throwing him a lifeline.

"Uh, yeah, I guess that's what I mean." He glared at Nina, who finally found her voice.

"Yes, the *Athena* was a much smaller ship. Boat actually. Kind of a yacht. The activities there were pretty much limited to stopping at all the Greek ports." There, that should give him enough information. No, wait, there was something else he should know. "And of course, once Steve proposed and that captain performed our marriage ceremony, we didn't spend a lot of time sightseeing." She glanced back at him to see if he had absorbed the wealth of information she had just conveyed in, she hoped, not too obvious a fashion.

He straightened in his chair and stared at her with a mixture of indignation and astonishment in his eyes. From the icy gaze he pinned on her, she suspected he didn't think much of her tale. Suddenly, it did feel a bit chilly out here in the open. She wished she had agreed to Ana's offer to fetch a sweater.

But at least her sister found nothing amiss with the recount of the whirlwind courtship. "It's such a romantic story," she sighed.

"Yes, very romantic. Almost like a fairy tale." The crispness in Grams' voice sent a wave of panic through Nina. But a searching glance of her grandmother's smiling face revealed no hint of disbelief or disappointment. In fact, Grams had her determined look. The one she wore when she was plotting something.

Nina shook her head. Her own plunge into plots and lies was making her imagine things. But she couldn't argue with the whisper of relief that slid through her when Ana and Grams finally decided to go to their cabin to rest. Wiping the moisture from her brow, she slumped in her chair.

As soon as he and Nina made their escape from her family, Steve grabbed Nina's wrist and tugged her to their cabin. When the door closed off the rest of the ship from them, he turned to her.

"That whole game of twenty questions, and you never once mentioned we supposedly married on a boat in the Greek Isles?" He bit the words out through clenched teeth. "Your whole plot could have been blown out of the water just now. For Pete's sake, what else haven't you told me?"

"I didn't think of it." She scowled as she paced around the small room. "I was thinking about questions they might ask, not about things I'd already told them."

"You didn't think of Greece?" He snorted. "I've never been there at all. What if I'd been asked what I liked best there?"

"So, you'd say the food. That's what everyone says." She hunched her shoulders and glared back at him.

Defiance tilted her chin. Obviously, she wasn't going to admit she'd messed up.

"Okay, fine. What do I care? This is your little scheme, your problem. If the house of cards comes tumbling down, it's no skin off my nose." With that mix of metaphors, he flung himself onto his bed. He picked up the ship's brochure and made a show of reviewing the amenities. Turning the knife, he added, "They probably have already guessed the whole story, anyway."

From the corner of his eye, he watched as she looked around the room uncertainly. Finally she sat on the other bed, facing him.

"Do you really think they suspect?"

The forlorn trace in her voice touched him. Rationally, he knew she should just reveal the whole lie and concentrate on having a good time with the people she loved. From what he'd seen of her grandmother, he was pretty sure the old lady would forgive her easily enough. Assuming she didn't already know, and that was a pretty big assumption.

But the sadness in her voice told him how important carrying on this scheme was to her. She was absolutely convinced that a solid belief in her granddaughter's happily married status was crucial to Grams' health and welfare. So maintaining the fiction of their marriage was crucial to her own happiness.

And her happiness had become important to him.

He really didn't want to think right now about why it seemed so necessary to remove the frown from her face. So instead, he just sat up and took her hand. Fighting the slow burn coiling in his gut at the warmth of her smooth skin between his hands, he stared deeply into the twin pools of liquid jade.

"Tell me everything you told them." Surely a recount of the fibs that had spilled from those beautifully formed lips would help him overcome this fatal attraction.

The next morning, as he walked with Nina toward the dining room at which they'd agreed to meet the others for breakfast, his head was still reeling. Tales of meeting in Innsbruck, him following her from city to city, nights on romantic islands, a sickeningly sappy proposal involving rose petals, champagne, and complicit waiters, a shipboard wedding ceremony that probably wouldn't even be legally binding, at least not in this country, and several months of marital bliss whirled through his brain. The fact that the bride had spent more than half of those months as the "Solitary Traveler" didn't seem to affect the credibility of the story to anyone but him.

He wished he had taken notes.

He hoped he could avoid dropping any more unintentional bombshells on Ana or Grams. Even though he thought Nina should come clean to her grandmother, he didn't want to force her to do it by messing up the game plan.

At least he knew who, what, where and when, even if he was having trouble with why.

"There you two are." Ana greeted them as they approached the table. "We were worried maybe you were going to have a romantic breakfast in your stateroom." She waggled her brows at them saucily.

Even as he grinned back and shook his head, the vision of an intimate meal in the small cabin he shared with Nina danced before Steve's eyes. It had been a long night, knowing the delectable woman was only a few feet away, dressed in only a long cotton T-shirt, in pale pink that should have clashed with her hair but instead simply made it more vibrant, breathing softly, occasionally sighing in her sleep.

And when she had awakened, her hair all sleep tousled, and her eyes heavy lidded from sleep, it had been even harder to act the gentleman. In truth, joining the other ladies for breakfast probably saved his sanity, even if it did mean risking more conversational pitfalls.

But before he could sit, Grams jumped up and took hold of his sleeve. "I want you to meet someone, Steve." She pulled him over to a table across the room, occupied by a gray-bearded man wearing a crew uniform. "Dr. Kendall, I want you to meet my grandson-in-law, Dr. Steve Tabor. He's the one I was telling you about."

Steve didn't allow any trace of the panic he felt show in his voice as he greeted the "other" doctor. He shook hands calmly, while his mind raced to find an excuse to end this conversation as quickly as possible.

"Good to meet you, son. Mrs. Anderson was telling me all about you and your bride." The older man smiled broadly. "She's very proud of you both."

"We're both very fond of her too." As long as the conversation stayed on topics like this, he could handle it pretty well.

"I understand you're a plastic surgeon."

Uh, oh. So much for safe topics. "Yes, but no shop talk! I'm on vacation, you know."

"Yes, yes. Your wife's grandmother told me it was a delayed honeymoon, eh?"

"Heh, heh. Right." His mind a total blank, he could do little more than nod. What did you say to a doctor if you didn't want the conversation to relate even remotely to medicine? "So, Doc, if you practice aboard ship, where do you go for your vacation?"

"I'm a ski bum every chance I get. Love Aspen."

"Never been much of a skier myself. Of course, that's heresy for anyone from Colorado to admit." He smiled and tried to think of something else to say as Grams patted his arm fondly. But he didn't have to worry. His new grandmother had the conversation planned.

"Steve, Dr. Kendall told me something that I think you and Nina will be interested to hear. Apparently the honeymoon suite is available!"

"Oh, really? That's odd." After the study session about his "courtship" of Nina, he had tried to upgrade the suite himself, but was told there was nothing free. Had the feisty septuagenarian beaten him to it? Over the old woman's head, he craned his neck toward Nina, now sitting beside her sister. Catching her attention, he managed by means of rolling his eyes wildly and jerkily nodding his head to convince her to join him. She approached just in time to hear Grams' great idea.

". . . so I think you and Nina should move into that suite. Much more appropriate for you two. Under the circumstances."

"Move into what suite?" The wariness in the red-head's voice had his heartfelt sympathy. Almost.

"Oh, honey, I have such a nice surprise for you! And I won't take no for an answer!"

"What have you done, Grams?" Panic sounded in the normally melodic tone.

"Now, sweetie, you know how you've just refused to let me buy you and Steve anything for your wedding present."

"No, Grams. I've told you, we don't need anything. Nothing at all."

So the redhead was willing to tell lies but not profit from them? Well, he had to give her credit for that. Most women he knew would have sucked up all the perks and worried about the fallout later.

But Grams was having none of it. "The two of you do need something. You need a proper suite for this cruise. The honeymoon suite was available, so I've already arranged for you to be moved into it. In fact, they should be moving your luggage now.

He wondered how the redhead would worm her way out of this one. A honeymoon suite wasn't going to have twin beds. He couldn't help but look forward to the two of them in a nice big bed. With the ship sway-ing provocatively beneath them.

He had to admit, he definitely liked Grams.

A jab of an elbow in his solar plexus ended his mus-ings. "Say something," hissed Nina.

Say something? What could he say? "Grams, you're a peach. But it's too much." Actually, it was probably much too much. Fancy suites couldn't come cheap on a ship like this. But no worries there. He'd just make sure he got the bill, not Nina's grandmother. Although come to think of it, he supposed that Rebecca Anderson wasn't exactly hurting for money, which made Nina's reluctance to accept expensive gifts all the more intriguing.

Nina was expanding on his theme. "Definitely too much. Thanks, Grams, but we just can't accept!"

"Nonsense! It's all arranged. Now sit down and eat your breakfast and then you can see your new cabin."

He glanced down into Nina's troubled green eyes. If ever there was a good time to reveal the truth, this was it. Her shoulders slumped and she looked the picture of guilt. But no confession burst through her lips. Instead, she meekly followed her grandmother to their own table.

He brought up the rear, trying to feel guilty about looking forward to the coming night.

Chapter Five

Breakfast over, she and Steve walked to their new cabin. She felt as though she were walking to her own execution chamber. She knew what the fancy suites cost. Grams had a comfortable income, but she had never believed in spoiling her grandchildren with outrageously expensive luxuries. Only a special gift, like a wedding present—for a real wedding—would justify an expenditure like this.

Pretending to be married was one thing, but accepting expensive gifts was quite another. How could she ever repay Grams for something this lavish? Or, at least, repay her without also telling her the truth about Steve?

As they stopped at their door, she let Steve take the key from her hand. It slid into the lock easily, and he pushed the door open. A sitting room with the sort of dainty furniture found in glossy magazines greeted them. The kind that made her want to check to make sure the seat of her pants wasn't dusty before she sat in them.

Steve looked around the room, the frown on his face doing little to mar the firm line of his jaw. "My first stepmother filled my father's house with impracticalities like this. Or maybe it was the second. Anyway, I never cared for it."

Nina blinked at the thought of having enough stepmothers to confuse them. Then she too looked around the room. She doubted the honeymoon suite would ever be featured in her "Solitary Traveler" column, but there was definitely plenty to see.

A huge basket of fruit and chocolates overpowered the small round table centered among the seating arrangement, while bowls of fresh flowers were scattered here and there. A tray containing a chilling magnum of champagne and two elegant flutes sat on another table.

He picked up the bottle to inspect the label. "No supermarket brand here. Definitely good stuff. These cruise lines don't kid around when it comes to luxury, huh?" He set the bottle down and picked up a card leaning against the crystal glasses. "Best Wishes from your cruise staff," he read aloud. He raised a glass with a questioning look at her, but she merely shook her head again.

Steve strode across the room to the fruit basket. Another card dangled from the bright gold ribbon and he read it aloud. "For Nina and Steve—Since you never had a real wedding trip, we thought you should have the honeymoon stateroom. It's our wedding present to you both. Best wishes, Grams and Ana."

"Ohhh, nooo. Not Ana, too." Nina covered her face with her hands and sank onto one of the little chairs. "Even that basket cost an arm and a leg. Oh, this is all so expensive. How can I ever pay them back?"

"Don't worry about that." The gruffness in his voice touched her.

She looked up at him, to find sympathy mixed with a touch of censure in his eyes." How can I not worry about it? They've given me a gift for a wedding that never took place. And even if I had gotten married, the cost of the honeymoon cabin would be too much." She'd only meant to please Grams. How had it gotten so out of control?

"I'll have the charges transferred to my credit card."

Her jaw dropped. She could only stare at him for a moment, before shaking her head. "That's really sweet of you, but I couldn't let you do that."

He shrugged his wide shoulders. "It's no big deal. Really. Money's never been an issue for me."

A warmth spread through her. What a great guy. Even if he apparently did have a wealthy family, there was no reason that wealth should be wasted because of her mess.

"No, thank you, but I can't accept it. I promised *you* a free cruise in return for helping me." She laughed at the irony, fighting tears. "Anyway, I can't pay them back without telling them the truth. I never meant for them to do something like this."

The wary expression men get when faced with tears crossed his face. He sank to one knee beside her and put an arm around her. "You could make it up to them, I suppose. Buy them something fancy in return. For Christmas or their birthdays." He waved one hand, palm up. "After all, with a rich celebrity plastic surgeon for a husband, you must be rolling in dough." He quirked a small smile at her, one brow raised hopefully.

Her laugh sounded pitiful to her own ears. But a different feeling began to work its way through her misery. Heat from his arm seeped through her thin cotton blouse. It felt rather nice to have his arm around her. Very nice, actually. She breathed in the combined scent of sandalwood and soap. His breath was warm on her cheek.

She'd have to find a way to pay Grams back. Maybe a bride's magazine would buy an article about cruising for honeymoons. She could earn enough to pay Grams back and pretend the magazine had picked up the tab for the stateroom.

She sighed. It seemed the lies just kept building.

Meanwhile, there were certainly worst fates than spending a week in the lap of luxury with this guy. She leaned against him, liking the sensation of a firm masculine body pressed against hers. This honeymoon suite was pretty nice, after all.

Honeymoon suite! A certain inevitable aspect of honeymoon suites occurred to her.

She jumped up and ran to the door that undoubtedly led to the bedroom. She looked inside and let out a screech that brought him running.

"Oh, no!" She slammed the door shut and turned to face him with her back pressed again the wooden panel. She stared at him, one hand clasped across her mouth.

She had been so concerned about the expense, she'd completely forgotten. Hot blood crept into her cheeks.

"Now what's wrong?"

He reached for the door handle, but she moved in front of it, shaking her head.

Gently pushing her aside, he opened the bedroom door and sucked in a breath as he walked inside.

Miserable, she trailed after him.

While the sitting area resembled a room straight out of Versailles, the bedroom décor clearly had a more sybaritic influence. The room was tailor-made for the willing seduction of a bride.

Instead of the chaste twin beds in their former cabin, a huge satin-covered bed dominated the room. Lengths of sheer fabric billowing around the bed nearly hid a basket of goodies waiting atop the pink spread. Closer inspection revealed more chocolate but this time in syrup form, colorful bottles of massage oils, votive candles, and a small cluster of pink feathers gathered with a ribbon.

Feathers?

Puzzling over that one, her gaze met his over the bed. Instantly a parade of images marched across her mind, with every love scene from every movie she'd ever seen vying for center stage. Except in her versions, instead of famous actresses, she seemed to be the one languorously stretched on the satin spread, dressed in a long silky gown trimmed with swansdown. Next came the picture of Steve leaning over her, smiling down at her, threatening to tickle her with the little bouquet of feathers.

She blinked. She looked back down at the basket. Wow. Feathers seemed to be pretty powerful stuff.

Glancing back at Steve, she saw him open his eyes, and groan softly. He quickly stepped into the sitting room. She followed him, trying to get her breathing under control.

He let loose a rueful laugh as he looked down into her eyes. "I guess that means I'm sleeping on the couch, huh?"

She appreciated his offer, but casting a glance at the delicate gilt furniture gracing the sitting area, she was pretty sure that boat wouldn't float.

Firmly placing the issue of sleeping arrangements on the back burner, Nina convinced herself the best way to avoid uncomfortable questions was to plunge into the ship's activities. They spent the rest of the morning at painting lessons, with the instructor thrilled to find a genuine artist among them. Then they joined the shore tour to Valdez in the afternoon. The river raft trip had been especially fun, proving a hit with everyone. Near escapes from death by crashing into submerged rocks, combined with breathtaking scenery, discouraged any dangerous discussions.

But tonight they would be sharing a late dinner with

Grams and Ana, and so conversational pitfalls loomed. On the way to the dining room, they reviewed their stories again.

Once again, their companions had preceded them. And two other couples, both looking to be in their fifties, were also at the table with her sister and grandmother.

"Hey, Nina and Steve! It's about time." Ana performed introductions, adding at the end that her brother-in-law was a doctor.

As the other passengers at the table greeted them, Nina ignored the inevitable snort emanating from Steve. She slid into her chair at the large round table, smiling over her shoulder as Steve pushed her chair in for her. Taking a deep breath, she turned to her fellow diners. "Hello, everyone."

"What kind of doctor are you, Steve?" The question came from Jessie, a Phyllis Diller look-alike across the table.

Steve rolled his eyes at Nina and took a large gulp of water.

"He's a plastic surgeon."

"No, really? A plastic surgeon? How wonderful," the improbably-blonde crone cooed. "You must be thrilled to think about getting your repair work for free, dearie."

Repair work? Too startled to reply, Nina could only stare at the woman.

But Steve was on his toes, apparently. "Nina isn't likely to be needing anything done ever. She has good bone structure." He smiled first for her alone and then included Grams and Ana. "Obviously runs in the family."

His protectiveness warmed her. And how sweet to

include her family in his compliment. She beamed at him.

"Bone structure? How does that help with laugh lines?"

"That's a good question, but I think I can explain." Steve took a gulp of water. "People are a lot like dogs. You have some breeds, like Afghans and Borzois with their long narrow noses and sculpted foreheads. Their hair and skin is laid delicately upon the bone structure, so they look sleek and elegant well into their golden years. And then you have pugs and pekes and bulldogs and such. Their bone structure, with shorter snouts, results in a bit more overlap of the skin and heavy jowls, so they look wrinkled even as pups.

"Heh, heh, Jessie, he's got you there." Jessie's husband cackled. "That little pug dog of yours could use a facelift, for sure. Maybe the Doc here could take a look at him before we dock."

"Howie! Shh! No one's supposed to know I brought Maxie—" Jessie stopped suddenly and glanced at the others at the table. Her eyes darted around the table as a guilty flush crept up her neck. "I mean, what a good idea. Doc, maybe you could give me your card, and I'll give you a call when we get home. Because Maxie is at home. Not here."

A short silence followed as the implication of this denial of a confession set in.

Trying to end the ensuing awkwardness, several voices were heard at once. "I have a cat named Sasha," said Nina.

Her sister chimed in, "I keep two parakeets in my apartment in New York."

"Our retriever is named Max, too." A man who'd introduced himself and his wife as the Olsens, stated. "Good name for a dog." He pointed a fork at Steve. "But do people really get plastic surgery for pets?"

"No, no. I was just giving an analogy." Steve frowned, obviously preoccupied at the thought of a dog aboard the ship.

"Oh, I see. So, what kind of surgery do you do most? Do you do a lot of implants?" The other man waggled his eyebrows suggestively.

"Now dear, remember, you promised, no shop talk!" The lie came out so smoothly Nina worried she was getting too good at it. Too much practice.

Pushing thoughts of her descent into a life of deception away, she smiled brightly and picked up the menu. "What is everyone having?"

Dinner progressed smoothly, with no further mention of Maxie or other dogs, and only the occasional embarrassing question put to the "newlyweds," when suddenly a shout was heard from across the dining room.

"Steve!"

The roast chicken Nina had just described as scrumptious turned to powder in her mouth as she watched a gorgeous blonde slink up to the table. The woman was wearing a skin-tight red sheath that started and ended only just this side of legal. The excess of makeup caked on her face couldn't hide exactly the kind of bone structure Steve had just been discussing—

the elegant sculptured cheekbones of a fashion model. In fact, Nina was pretty sure she'd seen this woman on a magazine cover.

Even though she already looked quite tall, four-inch heels forced the newcomer to bend low to plant a smacking kiss on Steve's lips. She followed that up with a tight hug, pulling Steve's face into her bounteous bosom.

"Sandra!" The strangled sound suggested Steve was being smothered by the attention. "What are you doing here?"

Fire shot up her spine at the sight of this temptress caressing him.

He's not really my husband. Nina told herself this sternly as she felt the hairs on her neck stand straight up. *Jealousy is out of the question. I barely know this man.* It would be wrong for her to scratch out the mascara-coated eyes. Very satisfying maybe, but wrong.

Still, she couldn't help but applaud inwardly when Jessie asked innocently, "A former patient of yours, Doc?" Nina had no problem categorizing Sandra amongst the female dogs in Steve's veterinarian life.

Jessie's husband added, "She's one fine advertisement of your work there, Doc."

Nina giggled, suddenly realizing the couple now thought Steve specialized in augmentation. The woman certainly could serve as an "after" picture.

But that thought made her cross her arms in front of her. She had never felt lacking in that department before, but the lady in red seemed to have plenty more besides what spilled over the top of her dress.

"Patient? Advertisement?" Obviously puzzled, the woman started to ask what the older couple meant, but Steve intervened.

In a harsh tone very unlike any Nina had heard from him, he asked again. "What are you doing here, Sandra?"

"Sandra Baxter! You're Sandra Baxter." That announcement came from Ana, who'd been frowning at the woman in concentration. "The swimmer. The Olympic medalist from a few years back."

Sandra sent a short dismissive glance her way. "That's right, honey, but no autographs, please."

Ana flushed. "No, I didn't want . . ."

But the swimming star turned back to Steve. "Why honey, when you told me you were going on a cruise, it occurred to me that this was just the thing for us all to get together and get past any unpleasantness. It certainly took a lot of calling around and pulling of strings. Do you know, the only way your new office was able to find out where you were was by checking one of the patients' charts? But anyway, we found out which cruise you were taking. And so here we are!"

Cold silence greeted this announcement, coupled with an even colder stare.

Nina hurriedly spoke up. "We? Are you with someone?"

Cold eyes assessed her and quickly dismissed her. "Not that it's any of your concern, but I am here with my fiancé."

"Oh, you're getting married. Congratulations! I'm

sure we wish you very well." She nudged his arm. "Don't we, Steve?"

He shook himself, and nodded slowly. "Yes. Yes, *we* do."

Sandra narrowed her eyes and looked from Nina back to Steve. "We?"

"We." A smile that didn't quite reach his eyes spread across his face. "This is my wife, Nina. Nina, this is Sandra. My *first* wife."

A gasp went around the table.

"Nina, you didn't tell us Steve had been married before." Grams' voice was reproving.

Ana stared intently at her sister before asking in a low, appalled voice. "You did know? Right?" The unspeakable implications of the question dripped so heavily from her tone they seemed to pool in the middle of the table like a sticky puddle of syrup.

Jessie's eyes lit up and she clutched her husband's arm. "Ooh, this is better than *All My Children*. And to think, Howie, you wanted to go to Las Vegas again!"

Nina closed her mouth with an effort. She hadn't known he was married before. But then, she hadn't asked. After all, what difference did it make for a pretend marriage anyway?

I'm out of the husband business. The words he'd spoken at their first meeting came back to her.

So this was his reason.

She'd always been one to give folks the benefit of the doubt, but this time Nina made an exception.

She did not like Sandra. But Jessie's excitement

notwithstanding, she wasn't going to play a part in an episode of a soap opera, either. This ship had paid entertainers.

She forced a laugh. "Of course I knew. What kind of question is that?" She waved a hand at Sandra. "I'm just amazed at how accurately Steve described her." There. That was a comment that could be taken a few different ways. If she personally leaned a bit more toward the catty meaning, so be it. It sure felt good to say it.

She then gave her brightest beam of a smile to Sandra, and added, "We're on our honeymoon."

Sandra closed her gaping jaw with a start. She glared at Nina for a moment before unnecessarily smoothing her hair back with a practiced gesture. Nina felt a stab of envy at the satiny perfection of the style. She forced her arms to stay crossed before her, resisting the impulse to pat her own defiant curls into some semblance of order.

"Married? Now, that is a surprise. But I do wonder why you never told your family about getting married." The acid in her voice would have eaten through the tablecloth, and probably through the table, too. "Worried they wouldn't approve?"

"Your family doesn't know you and Nina are married?" Once again, it was her own sister who asked the question that hovered on the lips of the avid onlookers. Jessie let loose an ecstatic gasp.

Her imagination failing when she needed it most, Nina peeped at Steve. Surely he could come up with some clever explanation for this lapse.

But Steve merely laughed. "Just what makes you think they don't know, Sandra? I doubt my mother spends much time updating you on the family news."

"Well, your mother doesn't talk to me at all." Cold blue eyes flicked over him, and bright red lips curved into a knowing smile. "But your brother does plenty of talking." She pushed her hair back again, and shifted her weight to show off the other long leg encased in silky sheer stockings.

Steve's eyes narrowed. "Winston's been talking to you?"

Grateful her own bare legs in their flat sandals were fully hidden by the table, Nina rushed in with yet another lie, "It's been a . . . pleasure to meet you, Sandra. I'm sure your fiancé is anxious for you to rejoin him." Hope rang clear and true in her voice.

"My fiancé has already gone to bed." Sandra raised her hand to caress Steve's cheek. "You remember how well I can tuck a man in, don't you?"

Steve brushed her fingers away. "I doubt there's a man in all of Dallas that doesn't remember, Sandra. Is that why you moved to Denver? You ran out of an opportunity for new conquests?"

"She's moving to Denver?" Nina asked without thinking.

"Oooh, it's gettin' real good now." Jessie propped her elbows on the table to enjoy the show better.

"Don't worry. She doesn't move in our circle." Steve took a sip of his drink, his knuckles white on his glass.

"You mean, you don't move in mine." She cast a disparaging glance at Nina. "I guess an experienced woman was too much for you, huh, Steve? Is that why you chose this little innocent? How long have you two been married anyway? The poor thing looks like she's still a virgin."

All eyes turned to Nina. She just knew her face was redder than this witch's dress. She slid down in her seat and stared at the plate in front of her.

Lordy. Could people tell something like that? Was there a big sign above her head or something? She glanced toward Steve and met his arrested gaze. She struggled for something, anything to say.

Surprisingly, rescue came from Jessie. "Doc, were you drunk when you got married the first time?" Clearly, in her view, nothing else would explain such a pairing. The rest of the women at the table indicated silent agreement with that opinion.

Except for Nina, to whom the explanation for Steve's attraction was rather blatantly displayed in the red outfit the woman must have had spray painted to her body. But the question broke the tension that had arisen at Sandra's bald accusation, bringing chuckles from those seated at the table, and a hiss from Sandra.

"No, I can't claim that excuse," came the dry retort.

Sandra finally sensed her lack of welcome. "We'll be seeing you around, Steve." She moved off, but not without a parting shot. "Good luck, dearie. You'll need it when he starts giving all his attention to his stupid mutt patients."

Now Nina laughed, as much from relief that Steve's ex had finally departed, as from Sandra's unknowing support of Steve's plastic surgeon identity.

"Mutt patients indeed! What a shrew!" While Jessie had seemed to have taken to Nina with some dislike at first, her loyalties had clearly switched by the end of this sensational encounter. "That woman makes Erica Kane look like Mother Theresa."

"Who's Erica Kane?" Apparently Ana wasn't the only one who didn't watch much TV, as her inquiring look was mirrored on more than one face at the table. After a stunned glance at her tablemates, Jessie immediately began regaling them with the entire history of her favorite soap opera. Tactfully, everyone pretended more interest in this topic than in the real life drama that had just been played for them.

Under the cover of Jessie's involved retelling of years of episodes, Nina whispered to Steve. "I'm sorry. It must have been painful to see her again." She knew that woman had hurt him. But she was so beautiful. Did he love her still?

"It was a surprise, that's all." His reply was clipped. He took a long swallow from his wineglass, staring at the lit candle in the center of the table.

As Jessie's voice droned on, Nina watched the man she called husband. In profile, his face, so open when met head on, was set along firm, almost harsh lines. A hint of shadow trailed along his jaw, bringing to mind the heroes in her favorite pirate movies. As he watched the flame, his eyes turned smoky. He looked angry, dangerous.

Sexy.

Could a man who had loved a woman with so much . . . experience, ever come to care for a woman with none? She tentatively reached out her hand toward him, but abruptly drew it back.

Wait a minute! What did she care? This was a one week deal. And the only experience she was looking for was to convince her grandmother she was in happily-ever-after land.

Steve finished his wine with a gulp, and turned toward her. "Care for a romantic stroll along the deck, my dear?"

Her heart quickened at the request. But as she looked at his lowered brows and tightened jaw, she saw more desire to escape the dining room than a wish to spend time with her.

She repressed the bubble of disappointment rising in her throat. After all, "romantic" fit the bill for the show for Grams. So she smiled her goodnights to the company and put her hand in his.

Alaska summers leave little time for moonlight. Even past ten o'clock at night, the sun still hovered well above the horizon. The ship glided along a rocky coastline, where patches of brilliant green interrupted the rich gray stretches of sheer rocky cliffs. Here and there, glistening streams of water cascaded to the surf below.

But Steve barely registered the savage beauty of the scene. His encounter with that savage beauty who had been his wife left his guts tied in knots, and his senses had little room for anything but self-disgust. And he couldn't help but recall her knowing look when she claimed he hadn't told his family about his supposed wedding. Why was she so sure of that? What had she meant by that comment about his brother?

Nina walked beside him, offering the occasional gasp of appreciation for the view. But more frequently she cast him questioning glances.

He knew the question. But she obviously wasn't finding the courage to ask him outright what kind of idiot married a woman like that.

Just as well. How could he answer, except that he was that kind of idiot? Or had been, anyway.

He saw Sandra so clearly now. But when he first met her, the athletic body, the flirtatious looks, perfect makeup, and seductive clothes, had bowled him over completely. When she had turned her feral smile on him, he thought he'd died and gone to heaven. Claiming an admiration for his desire to do useful work, like his mother before him, she made him feel he was the center of her universe, and he eagerly made her the center of his. With her, he'd felt he could finally bridge the gap between the two worlds his parents had shuttled him between all his life. Even his father had been thrilled to think of an Olympic medalist adding to the Tabor bloodline.

But as it turned out, Sandra had only seen him as the means of achieving a high class lifestyle. Perhaps because she'd won only a bronze, or perhaps because her personality could be so grating, she'd never won the endorsement contracts she'd hoped would make her rich. So she decided to marry money instead. Once wed, she no longer thought veterinary medicine was a proper calling for a Tabor.

In this, she had his father's and brother's unflagging support. His father would have been fine with his son being a professional hockey player—after the Olympics, of course. But when Steve had passed up his Olympic team berth to enter veterinary school instead, his father had pretty much disowned him. That Steve actually worked instead of simply living off his trust funds like his brother Winston just made things worse.

There'd been a brief reconciliation with the marriage to Sandra. Tabor senior had thought all his sport star hopes might be realized in the next generation with Sandra's athletic chromosomes added to the Tabor gene pool. But Steve had resisted Sandra's efforts to get him to abandon his practice; she'd taken out her anger in blatant flirtations that ultimately went further.

He'd tried. He stopped working late and rarely worked weekends. But she wanted all of his time and a man who had no career but merely led a life of leisure. After all, his trust funds would have financed such a life.

But he would have hated it.

So when she had finally crossed the line with his best friend, he ended the marriage. Only then did he learn that his best friend had been only one of many with whom the line had been crossed.

His insistence on a divorce had reopened the wound with his father. The elder Tabor simply blamed Steve for the infidelities and bemoaned the loss of a potential mother of champions.

"She's very pretty." Nina's voice, barely above a

whisper, broke through his thoughts. "Your wife, I mean."

"Ex-wife." He could take pleasure in those words, at least.

"Yes, well, anyway, she's really something."

"That she is." His response sounded like a growl to his own ears. He glanced down at her in time to see her bite her lower lip. "Sorry. I didn't mean to take it out on you."

She shook her head, her red hair blowing gently in the breeze. "It's okay. I don't blame you for being upset." She looked down at the deck. "How long were you married?"

"Three years."

"That's a long time."

Long time? It had been a lifetime. He only grunted in response.

"Uh, no kids, I guess?"

"No." He added, more softly, "No kids." Pity, that. If there had been children, at least his father would have gotten what he'd wanted. She must have heard the regret in his voice. "I'm sorry."

"Sorry?" He supposed he should be grateful. What would the chances have been for a child that would have been his? The casino on board the ship probably offered better odds. "Don't be. Believe me, kids would have been a big mistake for Sandy and me."

"Do you miss her very much?"

"Miss her?" He stopped short and looked her full in the face. Her eyes were wide, unclouded, but tinged with pity. He recoiled from the look he'd seen all too often back in Texas. Turning away from her, he gripped the railing of the deck until his knuckles shone white in the paling light. He looked out at the craggy cliffs of he shore, but saw nothing.

A man who didn't know his wife was a cheating liar was a fool, and everyone pitied fools. In the end, the embarrassed sympathy mirrored in every face in town had gone a long way toward convincing him to move to Denver.

Why didn't anyone believe that he was glad the marriage was over? That he wasn't suffering a broken heart?

"I do *not* miss her," he threw over his shoulder. He turned back to Nina. "I do not miss the hair color changing every month. I do not miss endless bills from Victoria's Secret. I do not miss tantrums or being dragged to boring parties." He waved his arms for emphasis, enjoying the freedom of actually talking about what he didn't miss. "I really do not miss seeing which one of my friends isn't meeting my eye this week."

As the meaning of his words sunk in, full lips formed a pert little 'O', while her eyes, so impossibly big to begin with, so much greener than the forests that dotted the shoreline, opened even wider. For a moment, the shock in her face distracted him from his litany of complaints. Was Sandra right? Was this beauty really so innocent?

But no. He remembered the worst thing about beautiful women. "Most of all, I don't miss the damn lies that came out of her scarlet-edged mouth every time she opened it."

Nina's gaze fell from his. Her arms crossed before her, and a pink tongue slipped out to wet her lips, bringing a low groan from within him.

Lies, he told himself. How many lies had tripped off that dainty little tongue?

He didn't care. He gripped her arms and brought her closer to him. As he lowered his head, he stared into the green pools that seemed to speak her emotions so clearly. Flecks of gold flickered within her irises, while a soft line of black outlined the jade circles.

Could he trust those eyes?

His lips touched hers, and a sigh escaped her, mingling with his own quickened breath. After the briefest of touches, he flicked his tongue along the silken crease. Soft, warm, trembling. After only a second's hesitation, her lips parted, inviting him to plunge through the depths of her mouth.

He groaned again, and gently pushed closer to her until the wall stopped their progress. He reveled in the answering moans she released as he explored every crevice of her tantalizingly warm mouth. His hands pulled her close, holding her firmly. Her eyelids slowly closed, dusky eyelids falling to flushed cheeks.

"Here the two love birds are! Oh, isn't that romantic!" The grating sound of Jessie's voice seemed to echo across the fjord.

Chapter Six

Sudden awareness returned to Nina. The cool inflexibility of the wall against her back presented a sharp contrast to the heated masculinity holding her so close. For a moment, she stood perfectly still, her lips still locked with Steve's. She opened one eyelid. A smoky orb mirrored her own shock.

Adjusting her one-eyed view a bit, she saw their erstwhile dinner companions, all crowded along the deck, broadly smiling at their romantic discovery. Her eyelid snapped shut again. The moan that now passed her lips did not have a hint of passion, but certainly contained a great deal of embarrassment.

She put both hands against Steve's chest and pushed hard. He stepped back, his hands dropping from their intimate positions. She stood straighter, adjusting the tail of her blouse that had somehow escaped the confines of her skirt's waistband. After the briefest glance at his face, her gaze fell to the painted planks of the deck beneath her feet.

What in the world had come over her? It wasn't like she'd never been kissed before. She had. Lots of times. Well, maybe not lots, but definitely some.

But kissing had never felt quite so . . . intimate. So . . . shared. So . . . right.

Right? What could be right about it? Nope. No way. Nothing special about that kiss. Definitely no sense of any particular connection. Not at all like what she very much feared might feel like love.

She was not in love.

She was not ever going to be in love. Love robbed you of your dreams.

But my, kissing Steve sure felt good.

"Hi!" For about the fiftieth time that day, she felt the hot flush staining her cheeks. Really, she spent so much time lately with her cheeks reddened from the inside, she needn't have bought that new blusher. "All finished with dinner?"

"Yes, dear. We were just going to take in one of the nightclub acts. It's one of my favorite stand-up comics." Grams grinned from ear to ear. "But you two don't need to join us."

A chorus of voices joined in the disinvitation to the nightclub. The group hustled between her and Steve, making laughing comments about young love.

Her grandmother's happy smile went a long way to relieving Nina's embarrassment. Nina craned her neck to watch the departing cluster. As soon as the group was out of earshot, she grasped Steve's arm.

"Did you see how happy she was?" She turned to him eagerly. "She really believes we're married!"

But no answering smile greeted her. "Yes, that was quite the convincing performance we put on just now. You almost had *me* persuaded with that kiss. You definitely made believers out of your grandmother and sister."

A hot denial sprang to her lips, but died unspoken. She hadn't been performing for Grams or Ana. Hadn't even known they was there. She hadn't known anyone was there, except for him. Hadn't thought about anything except that she wanted him to look at her the way she was sure he looked at that drop-dead gorgeous ex-wife of his.

And why would she want that?

No reason. In fact, she wouldn't want that. Couldn't want that. Ever.

But had *he* been acting? Could that kiss have just been for show? Judging by the distance he put between himself and her now that the crowd was out of eyesight, she guessed so.

"No, Steve, you deserve the credit there." She released a laugh just a little tinny to her ears. "You were great. Especially that bit with the roaming hands—that was a real nice touch."

That was true enough. A very nice touch. His hand pulling her close had sent wild shivers through her. And the feel of his tongue sliding smoothly between her lips—well! Her toes curled in her sandals just thinking about it.

If she were looking for a real husband, she was sure

Steve could provide the requisite conjugal bliss. In fact, if that is what went on behind the bedroom doors of married couples, she could almost understand her mother's sacrifice.

Almost. Not entirely. And she wasn't giving up her dreams just to be Mrs. Somebody. Nope, not her. Not ever.

Which was just as well, because this Mr. Somebody wasn't available for more than this little hoax, anyway. Judging by his reaction to the news that his ex-wife's fiancé was present, he was jealous. And jealousy meant he still had feelings for Sandra. And besides, he'd said right from the start he wasn't interested in anything permanent. Even though the woman he apparently still loved was marrying another man.

"Oh, no, Nina, the honors are all yours." His tone was a tad sour. "I haven't seen a performance that good since my divorce. In fact, I'd put you right up there with Sandra in that department!" His head shook slowly as he stepped up to the railing and braced his hands against it.

"Really? You mean the kiss?" She couldn't help being a little flattered at a favorable comparison to someone as obviously experienced as the former Mrs. Steve Tabor. "You really think so?"

"Oh, absolutely."

Her heart gave a little leap. But wait a minute. He had sounded a bit less than enthusiastic. In fact, his words were a bit strained, as though forced out of his mouth through clenched teeth.

"You're not just being nice, are you?" She held her breath.

"Nice?" He spoke the word as the meaning were unknown to him. "Nice about what?"

"About the kiss. About whether you liked it." Lord only knew why this was important, but it was.

He turned, one arm sill resting on the wooden railing. Head tilted, he peered at her. "You want to know whether I liked kissing you?" Disbelief tinged his voice.

Now it was her turn to stare out across the water. Or at just about anything to avoid his smoldering gaze.

"Uh, sure. I mean, since you've entered into the spirit of things so *heartily*, I wouldn't want you to be disappointed." She managed to keep most of her uncertainty out of her voice. "Or bored or anything."

"Maybe we should see how we like kissing each other when we know there's no one around to witness it?" His low deep tone draped over her, warming her despite the rising breeze. His suggestion definitely had some merit. She shivered anew at the memory of his invading tongue, and her own welcoming response.

On second thought, she wasn't sure she wanted to find out how much of that kiss had been acting and how much had been feeling.

So she shook her head slowly. "No. It's been kind of a long day. Maybe we should just go to bed."

Just go to bed? His arm slipped off the railing, causing him a momentary loss of balance. A part of him protested at the nonchalant invitation. But other parts of him were straining at the bit, so he wasn't listening to the boy scout in his head. This was an offer he couldn't refuse.

"Sure. Great." He held out his hand to her. After a moment's hesitation, she placed her slim hand in his.

Nina was silent during their walk to the stateroom. At least, he thought she was. He was so busily engaged in an internal argument, he wasn't really sure.

There was nothing wrong with what he—they— were about to do. They were grown-ups.

And after all, he told himself, hadn't he decided after his divorce that casual attachments were all he wanted? No more falling in love with beautiful faces, no more commitments, no more dreams of building a life with a good woman or of raising a family.

No more shattered hopes. No more betrayals.

So what if Nina was just another pretty faced liar? Since he knew that going in, he wasn't taking any risks, right? They could have a good time, and the two of them could walk away when it was over. In just another six short days. And five fantastic nights.

Besides, he argued, to give the lady credit, it wasn't like she hadn't laid it on the line up front to him. The whole point of this charade was her unwillingness to get tied down. And that innocent look was definitely just that—a look, nothing more. Otherwise, her invitation would surely not have been so offhand.

So why not have some fun? Why not see if he could reproduce the same moans that she had put out for an audience? Only this time, the moans would be just for him.

Because you're not that kind of guy.

He smiled with self-derision at the thought. No, he didn't used to be that kind. He'd had no intention of following his father's footsteps. But his days as Mr. Nice Guy were over. That ended the day he'd walked in on Sandra and Rick.

Now all he wanted was to have some fun. Some fun named Nina.

He opened the door of their suite and allowed Nina to precede him inside. She walked to the bedroom door, but stopped suddenly.

She twisted to face him, one hand at her face. "Oh, no. I forgot! There's only the one bed."

"Of course, there's—" The meaning of her words sank in. His heart just sank. She had said "just go to bed," not "go to bed together."

"Only one bed. And we need two beds. Or do we?" Despite his intellectual acceptance that he'd misread the invitation, he couldn't resist the hopeful question.

But she hadn't even heard. "You take it." She nodded in conclusion. "I'll take the couch."

They both looked at the dainty love seat.

Chivalrous habits die hard. He hoped the ship had some good masseurs, because to get the kinks out of his spine caused by a night on that couch, he'd definitely need a massage.

"No, I'll take the couch," he sighed. So much for "no more Mr. Nice Guy." But he couldn't take the bed and let her sleep on that hard little thing. Was it his imagination, or was the darn thing shrinking before their very eyes?

"Don't be silly. I promised you a bed, so you get a bed. Besides, you'll never fit on that thing."

He opened his mouth to respond, but shut it again.

She was certainly right about that one. Two of those little couches end-to-end wouldn't hold his height.

"Fine. But you won't fit either. I'll sleep on the floor."

"The floor? I couldn't let you do that after all you're doing for me. I'll take the floor."

"No." He didn't care how luxurious the carpet was, he wasn't letting her sleep on it.

"Oh." She looked around the room for inspiration. Her face lit up. "I know! We'll sneak a deck chair in here. They're very comfortable. People fall asleep on those all the time."

She dashed out the door, leaving him sputtering after her. Her unfailing optimism appealed to him, but sometimes her energy amazed him. He couldn't help but grin at the mental image of her dragging one of the unwieldy chairs into the elevator and down the corridor. She'd do it too.

But the vision of indignant stewards marching the chair back to the deck immediately followed. Good lord, she really would steal one of those chairs, wouldn't she? He could just picture the pair of them being thrown off the ship at the next port. While that would solve their sleeping arrangement, Nina would not be happy. Grams would be pretty upset too.

And making Nina happy seemed increasingly important to him. What's more, he rather liked Grams, and wouldn't like to see her put out.

Not that he wanted to examine the reasons for his concern for Nina and her relatives, of course. Instead, he flung the door to the corridor open, determined to stop the madcap before any of the ship's staff had to.

He only just managed to avoid colliding with the man standing behind the door, one hand upraised as though about to knock.

"Winston?" All thoughts of chasing Nina down fled at the sight of his older brother.

"Hey, Stevie." Winston Charles Tabor, III strolled into the room. With unerring instinct, he headed straight to the wet bar and examined the decanters. Sniffing the contents of one, he poured himself a healthy shot and tossed it back. Only after smacking his lips did he look back at Steve. "Glad I caught you, Bro."

Steve snapped his jaw shut, and pushed the door closed. Folding his arms over his chest, he leaned against the door. "Why are you here, Winston?"

Having refilled his glass, his brother pointed one finger at him and laughed. "Funny. Just what I was going to ask you. Oh, no, wait. I already heard. You're on your honeymoon."

"What if I am?"

"Yeah, right. Now, I can see you not telling Dad if you got married, given the circumstances. But not telling Mom? Not a chance. So who's the chick, why are you pretending you married her, and why in the world are you hiding away on this ship?"

"I'm doing a favor for a friend." There was no real harm in telling Winston the truth. As soon as he saw there was no angle in it for him, he wouldn't care. "It's a long story."

"I've got time. The casino won't extend me any more

credit, so I have nothing but time." His brother stared into the glass he'd refilled as he spoke.

"Yeah, now that you mention it, a cruise really doesn't seem your style."

"Now, see, that just shows how little you know me, Bro. I cruise all the time."

"Really?"

His brother chortled. "Well, usually not in a boat. But you know me. I can never say no to a woman. She wanted to come on a cruise, so here I am." He raised his glass in a mock toast.

Steve laughed. He could definitely relate. But as the dots began to connect, his eyes narrowed. "What woman?"

"Sandra, of course. Now that is one high maintenance lady." He poured another drink. "But she makes it worth a man's while."

"No. You are not serious." It couldn't be. Surely Winston wasn't marrying his own brother's ex-wife. "You and Sandra?"

His brother blinked back at him. "I thought you knew." His brow wrinkled. "She told me you did."

"I thought she was marrying Ri—" Steve stopped. He hadn't told anyone in his family the reasons he'd split from Sandra. Not even his mother, and certainly not his father or brother. He wasn't sure if it had been a misplaced sense of chivalry, or his own hurt pride that had kept him quiet. Besides, much as the old man got his goat, he hadn't been able to disillusion his father about the glorious Sandra.

Winston Charles Tabor, Jr., had been the classic nerd growing up. Picked on by all the jocks, he had been ashamed of his own lack of athletic prowess. Even though his mathematical genius had left all his high school tormenters in the dust in the world outside of high school, the old man longed for athletic success. Buying up a few sport franchises had satisfied his need for a time, but what he really wanted was a champion with the name of Tabor.

His first-born, Winston III, had been a disappointment from the start. Winston simply lacked any competitive spirit. Second-born Steve had shown more promise, even proven a hockey whiz on the powerhouse DU team. But Steve's sense of competition had directed him to veterinary school, which is far more difficult to get into than medical school. And much too coveted to pass up for the mere possibility of a spot on the Olympic team and a future pro contract.

Perhaps he should have told his father the truth about Sandra. But if he had, he might have found out it didn't matter to the old man. And he just didn't want to know his dad's obsession went that far. But now his brother was marrying her?

Winston cocked his head. "You thought she was marrying who?"

"Rich. I mean, I knew she was marrying someone rich. Loaded. I just didn't realize it was you." He had to think about this.

"Yeah, well, like I said, she is high maintenance. But I guess this way she doesn't have to change the monograms on the towels." Winston looked at him over the rim of the highball glass. "You okay with this?"

No, definitely not. But not for the reasons his brother thought. "Does that matter?"

"Not to me. Not much anyway." His brother shrugged. "Hey, nothing personal, Stevie, but it's making the old man happy. Some of us have been a bit less careful with our trust funds than others."

Steve nodded. Now it made sense. His brother lived the life of a wealthy playboy to the max. He'd been burning principle for a long time. Sandra would help burn through some more, but if Dad was happy, he'd pay the bills. Maybe even build up the trust fund again.

"Good luck. I guess." Maybe he could talk to the old man. Let him know the truth. Maybe he'd still bail Winston out.

"Hey, thanks. But where's your so-called bride?"

As though on cue, the door to the cabin swung open with a bang. Nina backed into the room, tugging on the wooden frame of a chaise lounge.

"I got one, Steve!" She grinned over her shoulder at him as she pulled the unwieldy chair into the room. "Now we're all set for the night."

Stifling a groan, Steve moved to help her with the chair. "I can't believe you actually took one of these."

"Well, sorry, but the floor just isn't appealing. This won't be the most comfortable way to spend the night, but it will get the job done."

A choking noise reminded Steve they weren't alone.

He turned to his brother, who looked as though he were about to have a convulsion.

"Winston," he started.

"Hey, no need to explain to me what you do with your bride. I'm just glad to see you've lightened up a bit." He swigged the last contents of the decanter and swayed to the still-open door. "Have a great night, kids." With a short wave of his hand, he lurched out the room.

"Who was that?" Nina asked, peering out into the hallway after him.

"It doesn't matter."

"Oh, was it someone else asking for free medical advice? I had no idea people did that so much."

"Something like that." He shook his head, examining the chaise that was to be his bed. "This doesn't look very sturdy."

"Oh, it's fine." She climbed into the chair and laid back. "See! I'll be—oof!" She yelped as the chaise collapsed under her. For a moment, she looked too stunned to speak, but then she began laughing.

He reached a hand out to help her up. "The floor will be fine. Get me a blanket and a pillow, and I'll move the furniture out of the way." Shrugging in defeat, she disappeared into the bedroom, while he lifted one of the dainty chairs and moved it across the room. He was leaning to push the love seat back when Nina returned, arms empty.

"Stop. You're sleeping on the bed." Her color was high and a mulish look shone in her eyes.

He held up his hand, palm facing her. "Look, Nina, I

appreciate it, but I can't let a lady sleep on the floor." He shrugged. "I just can't."

"I understand that. Because I can't let you sleep on the floor, either. So we'll just have to share the bed."

Her present stance, with arms crossed before her, and a determined set to her jaw, did not suggest a sharing of bodies as well as bed.

"Share the bed?"

"Sure! Like in that movie, what was it, where the couple is spending the night in a hotel where there is only one bed, so they rolled up a blanket to put between them." Nina chattered on happily, quite pleased with her suggestion.

"I don't think that's a good idea." Actually, he thought it was a great idea, but not in the way she had in mind. Didn't those two end up entwined?

"We share the bed or I take the floor." She lifted her chin and stared back at him challengingly.

Like his brother said, he couldn't say no to a lady. He gestured for her to precede him.

Instead, Nina grabbed his arm and pulled him into the bedroom. "See for yourself. We'll each have just as much room as if we had twins. More room than the separate beds we had before."

"Roominess isn't the problem." He waved his hand at the opulence surrounding them. Honeymooners would eat it up, but if the sleeping arrangements were platonic, he'd prefer less suggestive surroundings. "It's a question of . . . privacy." That was the most diplomatic way he could think of saying that sleeping close to her would prove too much for his willpower.

"No problem. I know just what we'll do. I saw this in another movie." She opened the closet door and pulled out a blanket. "We'll hang this down the middle of the bed, and you will have your side, and I'll have mine."

Funny, he liked old movies, too. Something else they had in common.

"Yeah, I know the film. But Clark Gable and Claudette Colbert had twin beds on either side of that blanket." Despite his objection, he moved to the bed to help her. He wasn't sure not being able to see her was going to make that big a difference, but it couldn't hurt.

"I have some safety pins in my bag. We'll pin the blanket to the bed curtains."

Within a few minutes, the blanket was stretched across the center of the bed, attached at each end to the sheer gauzy fabric draped over the canopy frame. The safety pins had come from the sewing kit she said she never traveled without. Once again, he could not resist the tug of admiration for her ability to make do in every situation. He couldn't help but be impressed at her resourcefulness.

"There!" Nina stood back and admired their handi-work. "Looks pretty good, don't you think?"

He nodded. Too good. But he wasn't looking at the bed. The last rays of the setting sun were stretching into their window, creating a fiery gold halo around her wild curls. Lit from behind, her figure was revealed through the diaphanous fabric of her skirt and blouse. The length of sheer bed curtain hanging between them lent an exotic hint of mystery, blurring the lines of her face to a dreamy quality.

His breath caught in his throat and he wrenched his eyes back to the bed. Their makeshift wall sagged a bit in the middle, but it did provide a barrier. He hoped the wispy fabric of the canopy would not yield to the weight of the blanket.

"I guess I'll get ready for bed." She grabbed a small case and slid into the bathroom.

He was ready for bed now. Much too ready.

Perhaps a dip in the pool would help. The channel through which they passed just might be cold enough, but the crew would likely frown on him jumping right over the side. Still, he stayed where he was, staring at the bed. He recounted the bones in a canine skeleton, trying to turn his thoughts from the woman who would share the bed with him.

All too soon, the bathroom door opened. He redirected his gaze toward the doorway. Nina appeared, and the blood began pounding in his ears. Her long tanned legs were almost fully bared for his inspection, as her pale pink T-shirt ended just inches below the tops of her thighs. She'd washed away the small touches of make-up she wore, revealing a fresh, healthy complexion. Freed of her customary ponytail, bounteous waves of red curls rounded her face. From the tips of her pink-painted toenails to the top of the springy curls, she exuded warm sexy femininity in a manner far surpassing the practiced wiles of his former wife.

He closed his eyes, struggling for control over his raging hormones. By the time he opened them, she had slipped beneath the covers, which gave him some breathing room.

Only some. Even sitting in bed with covers to her waist, she presented far too inviting a picture. Grabbing his own bag, he headed for the bathroom. Turning the water on full blast, he barely stopped to peel off his clothes before stepping beneath the spray of icy water.

When the internal burning had finally cooled, he stepped out. Finishing the mundane tasks of daily maintenance, he slid on the sweat pants he'd brought for sleeping, and stepped out into the bedroom.

Nina looked up from a magazine propped on her bent but mercifully covered legs. He watched her gaze travel down his body before meeting his eyes, and he felt the warmth returning to the limbs he'd tried so hard to freeze in the shower.

She smiled, and all memory of the chilly water left him. So much for cold showers.

He crossed to his side of the bed and slid in. The blanket hid her from his sight, although it was thin enough for him to see faint shadows of movement. He breathed a sigh of relief at the respite from sensory overload offered by the sight of Nina ready for bed. But then he inhaled her sweet scent—a subtle mixture of summer flowers and soap. Innocent, soothing, and refreshing. Like her.

A movement in the bed informed him that Nina was shifting a bit on the mattress, but he discovered this time that recitation of the anatomical parts of small pets was no help in keeping his mind off her body. A quick glance at the bedside table revealed no reading material, and he briefly contemplated getting up to retrieve the latest Tom Clancy novel he'd brought along. But that would mean risking another sight of the sunny temptress, so he decided to just go to sleep.

He flicked off the lamp on his side of the bed.

Eyes closed, he shifted down so his head met the pillow. Releasing a heavy sigh, he willed his body to relax.

A soft voice came from mere inches away. "Do you want me to turn my light out?"

"No, that's okay." He opened his eyes a bit as he replied. And then opened them wide. Very wide.

In fact, he didn't think his eyes had ever been as wide open as they were right now.

He could tell. His own reflection stared back at him from a mirror set into the recessed ceiling above the bed. And next to that reflection was a reflection of the sagging top of the blanket.

And next to that was the vision of Nina.

He shut his eyes and tried to slow his heartbeat. *I'm dreaming this.* Hope infused the thought, but when he chanced another look between squinting eyelids, the same vision met him.

"Uh, Nina?"

He watched her head turn slightly in his direction. "Yeah, Steve?"

He swallowed with difficulty. "Could you turn out your light, please?"

Chapter Seven

The down pillow was one of the most restful Nina had ever had. She pulled her arms around it tightly, burrowing deep into its softness.

Her articles focused more on the budget-minded traveler. In all her travels, she had never stayed in such opulent comfort. But the thought no sooner crossed her mind when she remembered why she was lying on such an extravagantly comfortable bed. Guilt flooded her as she thought of the expense of Grams' lavish "wedding" gift.

She would just have to find a way to make it up to Grams. Without Grams knowing.

She opened her eyes. The blanket strung above the bed was still in place. But after staring at it for a moment, she realized the difference. She was on Steve's side.

Oh, lordy.

She'd firmly repressed any inclination she'd ever had to pursue a romantic relationship. Her mother's example had proven the destructive power of love, and she had no intention of ever getting caught in its grip. And since she knew she would never be able to share intimacy with a man she didn't love, she made sure she never got close enough to fall head over heels.

But had her body instinctively sought masculine attention given the opportunity? Were her hormones trying to take a stand separate from her practical decision?

Well, that was just too bad. She was in charge of her own body, and her own life. Just because it felt really, really good to lie here in the arms of a guy who was incredibly sweet, and wonderfully sexy, was no reason to slam the door on her ambition. So what if little tingles were running up and down her spine—heck, up and down her whole body—from the way his warm breath tickled the nape of her neck?

For a wild moment, she wondered about the possibility of making her relationship with Steve a reality. They'd spent only a few days together, but they'd had a great time. She knew he thought she should confess everything to her grandmother, but otherwise, they seemed to agree on things. Having a husband like him wouldn't be so bad. It felt kind of right, even, to have a companion.

Oh, no. What was she thinking? She groaned and buried her face in her pillow again. She'd firmly repressed any inclination she'd ever had to pursue a romantic relationship. Her mother's example had proven the destructive power of love, and she had no intention of ever getting caught in its grip.

Besides, Steve was out of the husband business. And it wasn't like he'd shown any interest in her. His drop-dead gorgeous ex-wife probably starred in *his* dreams.

She might as well just wake up and smell the coffee. Carefully, trying hard not to stir the mattress too much, she crawled crab-like under the blanket to her own side. Finally, she lay back on the bed with a sigh of relief that turned to a stifled gasp as her head hit the mattress. She gingerly reached a hand under the blanket to retrieve her pillow.

Finally safe on her side of the bed she opened her eyes again. And saw herself in the mirror above the bed.

A shattering scream jerked Steve awake. Sitting bolt upright, he looked around for the source of the screech. What was wrong? Had Vikings attacked the ship? Had the Captain steered them into an iceberg?

Seeing no evidence of marauders, and nothing to indicate the ship had hit anything solid and was taking on water, at least not on his side of the room, he lifted up the blanket to peer over to Nina's side.

Nina stood next to the bed, her face as red as her hair. "What's wrong?"

Apparently unable to speak, she pointed up over his head. He followed the direction of her finger and saw the mirror.

"Oh, that."

" 'Oh that?' You knew about it?" Embarrassment forgotten, she frowned. "You let me go through that whole business of hanging this blanket and everything, with that mirror there?"

He flushed. It wasn't like he'd deliberately deceived her, after all. But he couldn't help but feel a bit uncomfortable, given her flying hair, not to mention braless state.

"I saw it last night. When I came to bed." He raised an eyebrow. "I kind of wondered if you had noticed it."

"Of course, I didn't notice it. So why didn't you say something."

A good question. Why hadn't he said anything? Because if he had, she would no doubt have wanted to try and cover it. Which would have meant he wouldn't have been able to see her prancing around in that skimpy T-shirt of hers.

Just like now.

He had seen Sandra in the most provocative of lingerie, the most exotic things to be found in lingerie shops and naughty novelty stores. He'd enjoyed the shows, true enough. But his oh-so gorgeous wife had never come close to being as flat out sexy as this copper-haired siren in nothing more than a pink T-shirt.

His mother was definitely wrong about pink and redheads.

"Well?" She expected some response.

"Because I was tired?" He grasped the explanation that fit his solution of the night before. "That's why I asked you to turn out your light. I wanted to go to sleep." Not exactly a lie. He had wanted to go to sleep.

He had wanted to do anything that would get his mind off the ache he felt for this woman.

"Oh." The fact that he'd asked for lights out had obviously escaped her memory. She seemed a bit nonplussed. She sat down on the bed again. "Well, I guess the blanket idea was kind of pointless, huh?"

He shrugged, hiding the fact his heart nearly stopped when she crossed one leg over the other, giving him a close up view of her smooth thigh.

"Uh, sorry about waking you."

"No problem." He had a feeling waking up with her would never be a problem.

"A mirror above the bed. That's, that's kind of racy, isn't it?" A faint blush colored her cheeks, and she peeked at him from beneath her lashes. "I mean, it's there to watch . . ." The pink darkened several shades.

The air went out of his lungs with a whoosh. Sandra had been right about one thing. His "bride" was definitely not accustomed to sharing a bed with a man. A woman so beautiful must have attracted males since she was old enough to cross the street without an adult. Why had she kept them at bay?

"You've never . . . ?" he raised his brows in place of completing the intimate question.

Apparently, the question made it impossible for her to look at him even through the curtain of eyelashes. Both feet primly on the floor, she turned away and shrugged one shoulder. "Never with a mirror above the bed." She glanced at him from the corner of her eye, and turned forward again as soon as their gazes met.

He chuckled at her evasion, not sure why he got such

a kick out of teasing her. "What about feathers? Ever use them?"

"What *do* you use feathers—" she turned eagerly toward him, but sudden embarrassment apparently prevented her from finishing the question. She stood and pointed to the door leading to their bathroom. "You want to take the shower first this morning?"

"No." He reached out and pulled her down so their faces were inches away. "I want to show you what I can do with feathers," he whispered.

Her eyes widened, but as he pulled her closer, and their lips met, her eyelashes fluttered down to rest on her cheeks. With only a slight hesitation, her lips parted at his touch. Gently at first, and then greedily, he tasted her.

A simple shift in position laid her out on the bed, with him above, and he plunged the depths of her mouth exploring her sweetness, reveling in the tentative return of pressure from her. When he finally ended the kiss, he gazed down at her and smiled. "You were right, you know. Cruises are a lot of fun." He drew his finger tenderly along her smooth cheek.

Her eyes slowly opened, revealing her dazed state. A tentative hand reached out for his face and stroked along the edge of his jaw.

"It's rough." Wonder filled her voice at the discovery of the texture of an unshaven face. "Like sandpaper."

He ruefully touched his chin. "I could shave. Wouldn't take a minute." He dropped a light kiss on her nose. "And then we'll find those feathers." He started to get up, hoping she'd urge him to return.

But no.

Awareness had returned to her expression. She pulled out of his embrace and scooted back across the bed. Landing safely on the floor on the other side, she crossed her arms before her.

"I think we have forgotten that this is a *pretend* marriage. Just why did you decide to come along on this cruise, anyway?"

He was sufficiently distracted by the way her crossed arms emphasized her curves to answer without reflection. "Mostly because of Sandra's phone call."

Her brow knit. "She called you? Why?"

He shrugged. "She told me she was getting married again."

"And because of that you decided to come on the cruise with me?" Her nose wrinkled in her effort to understand.

He wanted to kiss that pert nose again.

"Well, that's not the whole story. I—" He stopped. How could he explain what he didn't really understand himself? The threat of Sandra coming to Denver would not have chased him out of town. The truth was, he'd been looking for an excuse to help Nina. For an excuse to be with her. Why?

He thought he knew, but wasn't sure he liked the idea. "It's complicated."

"Yeah, I guess it is." She turned without another word and stepped into the bathroom.

The unhappiness in her voice confounded him. But he could hardly explain something he didn't really understand himself.

* * *

The ship's daily newsletter, slipped under their door, listed the events offered on the cruise each day. Both studiously making no mention of the events in the bedroom, Nina and Steve looked over the schedule while eating their breakfast in the sitting room.

The number of possibilities occurring at one time on this floating city boggled the mind. They could choose to drive a few golf balls with advice from a pro, shoot skeet, work out in the gym, gamble in the casino, or listen to lectures on topics ranging from planning for retirement to writing a mystery novel.

And that was just the morning schedule.

He favored the golf, but Nina nixed his plans.

"Married couples do things together," she pointed out. She took a large bite out of a cheese danish.

"You've obviously never been married." he replied, trying not to stare as she licked frosting from her lips. "But I guess that means you don't like golf?"

"It seems so silly, chasing a ball around with a stick." She wrinkled her nose.

The light sprinkling of freckles across the bridge of that pert little nose fascinated him. He had never realized how sexy freckles were.

"Hmm, doesn't that make half the sports in America silly? Anyway, there's no chasing here. You're just hitting the balls into the water."

She said nothing. Taking a sip of coffee, she raised her brows at him over the rim of her coffee cup.

"Okay, point taken. You choose." He stabbed a sausage with his fork and ate it.

"I don't know. What seems particularly honey-moony?"

He choked as the sausage went down the wrong way. When he could breathe again, it was his turn to raise his brows at her. "That activity isn't usually offered to groups. At least, not on a family ship." He leaned toward her suggestively, breathing in her jasmine scent. Forking up a bite of melon, he held it to her lips, smiling as she accepted it with wide eyes greener than any cat's. Setting down the fork, he brushed her fiery hair out of her eyes, marveling at the silken texture between her fingers. "But we can still indulge."

She drew back, gasping. "Now, none of that! You, you didn't think that was part of the deal, did you?"

He looked in the still wide eyes, the green now clouded almost gray in her confusion. He wondered if this straight shooter would feel obligated if he said he had expected it. What if that was the price of the masquerade?

But he banished the thought immediately. He didn't want her out of a misplaced sense of gratitude, or still worse, out of obligation. If they made love, it would be because she wanted it too. Because she wanted him.

So he answered honestly. "No. I didn't think that. But, I am hoping it."

Her pale pink lips formed an "O" and then closed again as she audibly swallowed. She cast a glance at the bedroom door. "I can't . . . I've never . . ." her words broke off as pink filled her cheeks.

He leaned close and placed a chaste kiss on the tip of her nose. "When the time is right, Nina." He sat back, and returned his attention to his breakfast. After a moment, she began eating too. Another minute passed before she suggested they go look for her grandmother and sister before making plans.

And so it went for the next two days. The honey-mooning couple spent most of their days with the bride's family. They swam and took a pottery class. They oohed and aahed over the savage Alaskan scenery. On a shore trip, they took a helicopter tour of a glacial lakefront. In the evenings, they danced, took in the floor shows, and once, even ventured into the casino. All under Grams' approving eye.

Steve was surprised at how easily he grew to like both Grams and Ana. Nina's sister was an intelligent, levelheaded, young woman. Every bit as beautiful, but very different in personality from the rash, outgoing Nina. Steve found himself thinking of her as the sister he'd never had.

And Grams? When Nina had first explained the cha-rade to him he vaguely thought her grandmother must be some sort of tyrant who bullied her granddaughters mercilessly and ruled their lives. Instead, she proved to be a bright, funny, loving matron, who clearly wanted only happiness for her loved ones. The ease with which she accepted him as one of those loved ones touched him.

Which made it all the more difficult to lie to her. But Nina was convinced that the truth would break Grams' heart, so they maintained the pretence.

At night, Steve sweated through cool nights lying

only inches from her. Even Nina's ingenuity had been outwitted by the mirror—no sheet or beach towel she pinned up stayed for more than a few minutes. The last attempt had brought down half the sheer draperies as well, which spelled the end of the dividing blanket.

He wondered if the ship would charge them for the damage to the bed. Or were they used to repairing that article in the honeymoon suite?

Nina never asked him to sleep elsewhere, nor did she attempt to do so herself. But neither did she indicate that she would welcome him on her side of the bed, blanket or no blanket.

Except in her sleep, when she rolled easily into his arms. He never even considered taking advantage of the unspoken trust she showed him. So he held her close, but did no more.

But the ship was undoubtedly experiencing an unprecedented use of cold water in its honeymoon cabin.

On the fifth day of the cruise, Steve found himself under a huge glass ceiling that could be opened as the day warmed. A series of pools, whirlpools, and even a few waterfalls graced the area. Since the whole setup was not very far from his initial image of the cruise, he really didn't mind missing golf.

Lying on the lounge chair next to him, Nina filled out her bikini.

"Could you rub sun block on my back, please?" She squinted over at him, shaking the plastic bottle.

He glanced up at the glass roof. UV rays don't penetrate glass, so unless and until the crew rolled the top off, no sun block was needed. But he was not pretending to be a dermatologist, after all, so he took the bottle with a grin. At least *some* of his fantasies were coming true.

Nina rolled onto her stomach and lifted her ponytail away from her neck. Her back, peachy with just enough freckles to stir his blood, was bare save for a thin band of fabric just under her shoulder blades.

He took a deep breath and let it out slowly.

He knelt beside her and squirted some of the lotion into his palm. Rubbing the cool cream between his hands to warm it, he smoothed it over Nina's shoulders, then down to the strap of her bikini top. His hands turned in slow circles, watching as the liquid disappeared. He repeated the ritual of bottle squeezing and hand rubbing, and then moved to the small of her back.

Her skin fulfilled every silky promise. As he massaged the lotion in, he felt her first tense and then relax as she gave in to his ministrations. A low moan escaped her lips. With difficulty, he managed to keep his own answering moan behind his teeth. He wasn't sure this was such a good idea, after all.

"Well, well! If it isn't the newlyweds! Mind if I sit here next to you?"

Nina tensed as the drawling accent of Steve's exwife penetrated the warm haze that had settled on her brain. The hand at the base of her spine stilled for a moment, then resumed its languorous path.

"Morning, Sandra." His abrupt tone suggested it wasn't a *good* morning he wished on her.

Nina pushed herself up on her arms and turned to

face the vamp now draped across the lounge chair Steve had abandoned. She allowed an artificial smile to cross her lips, not showing the wariness that bubbled up inside.

"Beautiful day, huh?" Sandra sipped her drink. Her sharp gaze flitted from one face to another. "So just when did you two meet anyway?"

"About a ye—" Sudden pressure on her hip caused Nina to stop in the midst of her reply. She turned her head toward him and caught the slight shake of his head.

"A while ago. Why do you ask?"

The seductress' sharp gaze settled on Nina for a long moment before she let loose with her tinkling laugh again. "Just curious. You see, I can't help but wonder, since our divorce isn't really that old."

The hair on Nina's neck rose. She twisted around to sit up.

When had they gotten their divorce? Was it after the date she'd told Grams about the wedding? Would Sandra let it out that she and Steve couldn't be married?

"Our marriage was over long before the divorce was final. You know that." He turned his attention to Nina. "Honey, do you want me to do your front now?"

But the vamp wasn't giving up. "Oh, I know the marriage had lost its zing—for me anyway. But I hope you didn't marry this sweet thing on the rebound." She smiled like a cat full of canary. "I know finding Rick and me together like that, well, that must have been a shock." With that parting shot, she slithered away toward the bar.

As the vicious words sunk in, Nina peeped at Steve from under her eyelashes.

He'd actually *found* his wife with another man? Yowza! He must have been terribly hurt.

Did he still love his cheating wife? He must, if the knowledge of her remarriage is what had sent him running from Denver onto this cruise. He couldn't face the thought of it.

She could tell nothing from his face. All his concentration was on the tube in his hands. He gave a sharp squeeze, spilling the lotion out into his hand in a large puddle. Muttering beneath his breath, he clasped his hands together briefly and then smeared the gobs onto her legs. She jumped a bit at the cool feel of the cream, but warmth quickly suffused her legs with his vigorous rubbing.

She felt a deep stab of anger at the cool cruelty she had just witnessed. From the corner of her eye, she saw the blond peer at them over her drink. That woman was not the right one for Steve, but for some reason she seemed far too interested in him. If she was convinced his new marriage was happy, would she leave him alone? Then Steve could get over his ex and move on.

To her?

Nope, not what she wanted. She was just being altruistic, that's all. He was a nice guy and deserved better than this shark of a woman.

Acting on instinct, Nina reached out and cupped Steve's face, giving him the most sensuous smile she could muster. Leaning close, she whispered. "She's watching us. Let's show her how little you care about her." She feared he cared all too much, but if he wanted an opportunity to recover his pride, she was more than willing to give him a hand.

His eyes widened at her suggestion, and she had to hold his chin to keep him from looking toward his ex-wife. But after only the slightest hesitation, he gave a short nod.

"Do you mean what I think you mean? Sweetheart?" He reached up and stroked the top of her hand.

Funny how a heart could leap at even a pretend endearment.

She continued stroking his cheek. "Well, after all, here you are, with your new wife, at least she thinks so, and while you are actually spending time with the woman she thinks you married, there she is, all by her lonesome, watching us." Not that a tramp like Sandra was likely to be alone for long, but somehow, she didn't think he'd want to hear that. "She might like to think you did something you'll regret, but I doubt she's going to want to watch you having a good time with your new love." And if that didn't work, they could try shark repellant.

He still rubbed sun block into her skin, but his movements had slowed, becoming more sensuous.

"So you think playing the happy couple will drive Sandra nuts?"

She pulled her thoughts away from the feel of his thigh pressed against hers. The hair on his leg didn't quite tickle, but managed to send tingles up and down her spine.

What had he said? Drive her nuts? Uh, oh. Making

Sandra jealous was not the plan. She'd just been thinking that playing the happy couple would make Sandra see she couldn't torture him anymore.

But the rigid anger had left his face, replaced by that devilish grin she had grown to anticipate. So she smiled again, and said. "That's the ticket."

An hour or so later, she had to admit Steve had been right. Sandra was sticking to them like glue, but she no longer appeared the calm, cool, and collected socialite. She hung by the bar for a while, but she soon joined them again, sitting next to Nina and offering to dish about Steve.

Clearly the vamp didn't like the thought of her victim recovering nicely. But the longer she stayed, the more Steve played Romeo to the hilt.

And Nina was starting to like it a little too much. She'd made her career being the 'Solitary Traveler,' but she couldn't help but notice how easy it was to get used to a handsome man catering to her every whim.

Very easy.

So she was grateful when her sister and grandmother finally walked into the pool area. She waved them over to where she and Steve still reclined.

"Good morning, you two!" Grams bustled up, Ana serenely pulling up the rear. "You look like you both are sleeping well." The roguish twinkle in her eyes made the diminutive woman look like an elf, especially with her sensible bathing cap exposing her ears. "Admit it. That honeymoon suite was much more to your taste than single beds."

Nina exchanged a glance with Steve, who merely

flashed his gleaming teeth back at her. She felt a burning flush rise up her neck at the memory of just how much she liked sharing a bed with him. She felt powerless to answer her grandmother.

"Good morning, Grams. The suite is great—I've never slept so well as I do here. And it looks like the sea air is agreeing with you two, as well."

Nina appreciated his hearty tone. But seeing her sister in a bikini, with the only thing more shocking than the bright pink color its extreme shortage of fabric, she could have done with less enthusiasm.

Lordy, now she was jealous of her own sister?

"Wow, Ana! You sure look, um, different." When had her little sister grown up so much? But she had no more time to wonder about her mousy sister's transformation. Sandra was moving in for another sniper attack.

"Grams? Steve honey, you took your wife's grandmother on your honeymoon?"

Ana's eyes narrowed at the intrusion, and she gamely rose to the defense of her sister. "Well, it's not exactly a honeymoon. They've been married awhi—"

"Hey, is that a whale out there?" Steve pointed out toward the broad expanse of ocean before them. Everyone scanned the sea for a sight of a broad tail or water spouting from a blowhole. Even Sandra craned her neck for a glimpse of the rare humpbacks said to travel in these waters. But she gave up first.

"I don't see anything. Now tell me, are you on a honeymoon or not?"

"Well, not that I think it's any of your business, but Steve and I did have a bit of time alone together before we headed on this trip." That wasn't even a lie. They'd been alone in the cab ride to the airport. "It was a really nice surprise for Grams and Ana to be here." Well, it had been a surprise when Ana *told* her they would be there. But she knew her sister wouldn't give her away.

"Oh?" A carefully penciled eyebrow rose. "What did you think of that little surprise, Steve?"

Steve put his arm around Nina. He smiled down into her eyes, giving her a secret wink. "You know, now that I've met Grams and Ana, I just can't imagine coming on the cruise without them." And in a dryer tone, "And I know my mother will love them all too."

From Sandra's flush, his mother had obviously detested her former daughter-in-law. "How about your father?" she shot back. "Think he'll be pleased at your second choice?"

The malice in Sandra's voice startled Nina. What could she mean?

Steve rose from his place at Nina's feet. "I doubt I'll have to subject them to that introduction. Now, ladies," he clearly excluded Sandra from that title, "it's occurred to me that we should plan our shore trip tomorrow. We don't want to miss out on the great things to see in Juneau. I'll head over to the cruise director's office and bring back the flyers so we can choose what the *four* of us would like to do." His slight emphasis made clear that Sandra would not be invited to accompany them. He sauntered off.

"You never said Steve was so attentive!" Ana gushed as he went off. "It's so romantic."

"Romantic." A most unladylike snort issued from

Sandra. "I'm just amazed you got him to take time away from those mutts of his."

"Really, dear, don't you think you are being a bit harsh on his patients?" Grams' voice managed to be both soothing and admonishing.

"You've got to be kidding? Believe me—"

"Sandra, why are you so interested in your old husband?" Nina had finally had enough of this fifth wheel, who was all too likely to give away the game without even knowing it. "Surely your fiancé would object to you hanging around Steve."

Again the thin eyebrows raised. "Actually, my fiancé is every bit as interested in Steve as I am. And mighty interested in this sudden marriage of his." With those words, she flounced off in the same direction as Steve.

Ana watched the older woman slink away. "What do you suppose she meant by that?"

"I imagine any fiancé would be interested in a man his ex-wife can't seem to stay away from." Grams spoke in her driest tone.

"It is kind of odd," Ana agreed. "Gosh, Nina. I can't imagine having to put up with an ex-wife along on a vacation."

Especially a gorgeous ex-wife. One he wanted to drive crazy with jealousy.

A small voice inside Nina suggested he was succeeding, but with the wrong victim. But she brushed that voice aside and brightly asked her family about all the hometown gossip, completely forgetting how this topic had been exhausted already. Before long, Grams headed off to swim her daily laps, telling her granddaughters she'd be happy with whatever shore tour they chose.

Nina and Ana wandered over to the pool-side bar. It was the first chance the sisters had had to talk alone.

"Well, I have to hand it to you, Sis." Ana took a deep swallow of her colorful fruit drink. "To tell you the truth, I kind of thought you'd show up here alone."

"Alone?" Nina stared across the table at her sister as she absently snagged a couple of peanuts from the dish sitting on the bar. "You didn't think Steve would join me?" A quick toss sent the peanuts into her mouth.

"The whole reason I spoiled Grams' surprise reunion idea was because I didn't think you really had a husband. I figured I'd give you a chance to come up with some excuse to explain away his absence."

Nina coughed so hard, her sister had to slap her on the back. She took a huge swallow of her drink. Finally able to breath again, she let a nervous giggle escape before she clamped her lips shut. After a long moment, she asked, "Why would you think I'd make it all up?"

"Well, I never believed you'd actually tied the knot. You always talked about how you never wanted to give up your career. Even when we were kids you said you didn't want to ever get married."

"Oh, that." She avoided looking her sister in the eye by waving a waiter to the table. "Could we have more drinks, please? And how about some more munchies?"

"Yeah, that."

They stayed silent as the waiter poured margaritas for them each. Setting a basket of chips beside them, the waiter moved to another table. Smiling her thanks,

Ana continued, "When you suddenly announced you'd gotten married, well, I kind of figured you might have been making it up."

"Making it up. You though I was making Steve up." Even though her sister's suspicion had been on the money, Nina couldn't help feeling just a tad indignant. "You thought I was lying to Grams, to you, to everyone. Well, thanks a lot." She knew she was being illogical, but somehow it stung to think she had been less than convincing. Was she really such a bad liar?

Anyway, was it really lying when you did it for a good cause? She knew the answer to that question, but still, didn't good intentions count for something? Grams was so happy. Could she really regret it?

"Gee, Sis, don't get so upset. I knew why you would do it, after all. When Grams gets on her 'experience all life has to offer' and then starts in on the 'children are a joy you can't pass up' stuff, she's pretty hard to resist. She's even been trying to fix me up with some of the guys around here."

"Really?" Nina latched on to the possibility of another topic. "Have you met anyone you like?" Unlike herself, her sister had always been open to the possibility of marriage. She just hadn't found the right guy.

"Well, there is one guy I kind of like. He reminds me of Cary Grant." Ana giggled. "Very charming." She frowned. "But no changing the subject. Back to you. I only thought you might have made it up because sometimes I think you'd do anything, no matter how off the wall, just to make Grams happy."

"Well, I would." Somehow, the thought just made her

feel glum. How was she going to keep making Grams happy? How long could this go on?

A frown traveled across her sister's face. A hand reached across to clasp her own. "Nina! You didn't marry Steve just to please Grams, did you?"

"No! Of course not!" At last. A question she could answer honestly, if misleadingly.

Ana breathed a relieved sigh. "You had me worried there for a second. Grams would like to see us both find the loves of our lives, but she wouldn't want us to marry just for the sake of marrying."

"Are you sure of that?" There was just enough bitterness in her own voice to shock Nina. It shocked her sister, too.

"How can you ask that? You know Grams wants us to be happy?"

"But why does she think that happiness comes only from being married?" She took a deep swallow and sat back. "Honestly, how happy do you suppose Mother was, giving up all her dreams?"

"Well, I don't remember her much. I was only four when the accident happened. Mom and Papa both seem happy in my memories, but I was a little kid." She shook her head. "Anyway, no one made her give up her skating, Nina. Grams always said that it was her own choice."

"Her own choice. Right. How could it have been her own choice, when she had two kids and a husband to take care of?"

Her sister shrugged. "Having two kids and a wife to take care of didn't stop Papa. He kept up his career right until the end."

"I know. And I was old enough to see how tight Mom's smile seemed when she applauded him. I saw the longing in her eyes." She sat back. "Anyway, it's different for men. People expect different things from them." Nina stared darkly into the pink swirl of her frozen drink.

"Sounds to me like you're the one with different expectations." Ana popped the cherry that had floated in her drink into her mouth. "So does that mean you are going to give up being the 'Solitary Traveler?' "

"No, of course not!" Nina slammed her glass down on the table. "I worked very hard to make a name for myself. I won't throw it away for any man."

"Well, then. There you have it. Obviously Steve agrees with you."

"Why should he care?" She rubbed the salt of the chips from her fingers. Looking up, she saw her sister's dark brows raised high. Realizing her gaffe, she hurried to offer an explanation. "I mean, he's busy with his schedule, so he doesn't need to worry about mine."

Although, now that she thought about it, that could be what leads to the inevitable "breakup" between Steve and her. Because, came the miserable reflection, once this cruise was over, Ana and Grams would expect to see them a lot more. She was going to have to explain his absence. Lordy, as if the web she'd woven wasn't tangled enough. It was pretty much a humongous knot.

"Well, I'm glad to hear it. I think Steve is terrific, but I would have hated you giving up your writing. I like having a famous sister."

"You're pretty famous yourself. And you get to go to all those games."

"Huh! Like you wish you could go to games."

"Well, I wouldn't like it, but you can't tell me you don't." Her sister smiled in acquiescence. "Anyway neither one of us is famous like Mom or Papa. Or even like Grams."

"Trust me, *no one* knows the names of the sports photographers. And maybe there's no Olympic competition for travel writers, but you've still made a name for yourself. Although, personally, I think you ought to consider writing about traveling as a couple. You certainly seem to be having fun."

She was having fun. And that was a problem.

She had never expected to enjoy having a companion on her travels so much. She'd always liked the freedom of doing whatever she liked on trips, never having to think about someone else's feelings.

But it wasn't so bad to hear another opinion on whether to choose between swimming and watercolors. To eat in the formal dining room or to pick up a snack from the bar. Or have room service. Steve listened to her thoughts, presented his own, and they made a mutual decision. He never made her feel obligated to give in to what he wanted. Sure, sometimes she went along with his wishes, but sometimes, he went along with hers.

Sometimes it was even nice to just let someone else decide. Especially when the someone else was Steve. Maybe he'd like to come along on the series of trips she planned to explore the hot springs in the Rocky Mountains, she mused.

Whoa! Nina stopped that line of thought cold. Steve was along for the ride for one week only. That was the deal. And while he'd shown some interest in exploring *her*, he hadn't any in exploring the world *with* her. Except when there was an audience.

And that's exactly how she wanted it. Didn't she? She *was* the 'Solitary Traveler,' after all.

"I should get to work on the article today." She swirled a spoon through the dregs of her Margarita, making no move to head for her laptop. She'd been so busy she had not even started her writing. That was definitely unlike her.

Sheesh, even *pretending* to be married was interfering with her career. But somehow, she just didn't feel like extolling the virtues of sightseeing for singles right now.

Chapter Eight

Steve headed to the cruise director's office. There had to be some tour or something they could go on to get away from his ex. Obviously, Winston's willingness to marry Sandra for the sake of more cash from Dad did not include any obligation to entertain her on this trip.

He just couldn't believe his luck. He starts a new life far away from Texas, and winds up stuck on a boat where every time he turns around, his ex-wife appears. Why in the world had she taken the trouble to hunt him down anyway?

He turned a corner and ran smack into his brother. A petite brunette in a more petite bikini hung on the older Tabor's arm.

"Hey, Steve. Great idea, this cruise. I'm having a terrific time."

"Winston! Pay a little attention to your fiancé, will you? She's driving me nuts."

"Fiancé?" The brunette unlatched herself from Winston's side. Casting him a fierce glower, she tossed her head and sashayed away.

"Stevie, boy, that wasn't nice," his brother pouted.

"Nice? You call hanging with some bimbo behind the back of the woman you intend to marry *nice?*"

"I thought you knew the woman I intend to marry *is* the bimbo." He shot a wistful look at the retreating young woman. "That was a very nice young lady. And this boat is filled with them."

"So break if off with Sandra. Let her find some other meal ticket."

"No can do, Bro. I need a meal ticket too. Sandra may be an irritating jezebel, but she does have that all-important bronze medal. You know how important sports are to Dad."

"So maybe he should marry Sandra."

"Now, now, none of that. We don't want any more siblings showing up to dilute the inheritance!" Winston grinned, but the smile didn't match his eyes. To Steve, he looked like a man facing a noose.

"You could always get a job."

"Sorry. But you inherited all the responsible genes. Anyway, as long as Dad is happy, I'm happy."

"You don't look happy, man."

"That's because I haven't had my morning cocktails yet. But I believe there is a bar right this way. Later, Bro." He sauntered off.

Only his brother could save himself. Steve knew that. But it was with a heavy heart that he turned and walked into the cruise director's office.

"Hey, Doctor Tabor! Just the man I wanted to see."

Steve stifled a curse as one of the passengers who had shared their table last night approached him. He knew from his experience over the last few days that he was about to hear a litany of symptoms. He held up a hand to forestall the medical history.

"Sorry, Mr. Maxwell, but you know my feelings on this. I don't poach on another doctor's territory. Go see Dr. Kendall. He'll help you out."

As the portly man made his way out again, Steve shook his head. Judging by his own sudden popularity, people obviously did not go on a cruise for privacy. Maybe he'd take Nina to the mountains for their real honeymoon.

Whoa! Where did that come from? What honeymoon?

But the thought of a real honeymoon with Nina, with no blanket separating the two of them in bed, would not be pushed out of his mind. In fact, the thought of having that warm, generous spirit in his life on a full time basis started to seem downright attractive. Necessary, in fact.

Maybe he was crazy falling for a woman he'd known a scant four days. But then again, maybe the folks who lived together first had an advantage—there was no better way to get to know someone than to spend time in close quarters. His image of her as a scatterbrained liar had pretty much disappeared the first day. Instead, she was a warm, giving, loving woman who had a good sense of herself, and a good feel for the people around her.

True, she tried a bit too hard to please other people,

which is what led to the current masquerade. But that was the only fault he could find with her. Even her restless energy had grown on him. He'd felt more alive in the past few days than he had for as long as he could remember.

Nina might have a problem with the truth when it came to her grandmother's happiness, but he couldn't imagine her lying for her own advantage. And she obviously wasn't the sort who would ever sleep around. In fact, the only explanation for her innocence that he could think of had to be her reluctance to play without commitment.

But she wasn't willing to commit, at all.

Was she?

She had lapped up all the attention he lavished on her in front of Sandra. Maybe she wasn't completely immune to the advantages of a long term relationship. Playing Mr. Perfect Husband in front of Grams was all well and good, but he should try it without the audience. Maybe he could convince her to make the lie a truth.

Grabbing up the fliers for the Juneau tours, he headed out the door, stopping only to make sure the cost of the honeymoon suite was transferred to his own credit card.

Steve began his wooing in wily fashion. It had taken the merest hint that Grams might still be suspicious about their marital bliss to convince Nina to engage in some one-on-one amusements. So with the following day reserved for a family trip to Juneau, Steve had Nina to himself for the remainder of the day.

They ran around the jogging track together, followed by a soak in the hot tub. A healthy lunch came next. He then challenged her to a game of pool. They walked away from the game hand-in-hand, with Steve convinced she could easily make a living as a pool shark. She didn't make every shot, but a man was all too easily distracted by the sight of her bending over the table, her pretty pink tongue pressed against her upper lip as she concentrated on the angles.

But the crowning stroke of genius had been signing up for the "Couple Compatibility" game. Patterned after the old television program *The Newlywed Game,* participants were asked to write down answers to a list of questions about their own likes, dislikes, and desires. To discourage any idea of cheating, the men were sent to one side of the mini arena to answer their questions, while the women were sent to another. The idea then was for the score keepers to reveal how well—or how little—the pair matched up.

After turning in their score cards, they sat to listen to the Master of Ceremonies. The cruise employee was dressed in a bright white T-shirt paired with swimming trunks decorated with hearts. He interspersed his corny jokes with good-natured teasing of the passengers.

"Okay, now. Next, Bill and Edie have been married for, what? How many years? Thirty years, ladies and gentlemen, let's give them a hand."

Steve and Nina joined in the cheers and applause. The honored couple blushed and waved in embarrassment.

The M.C. continued, "Well, these two really ought to know each other, huh? But, oh oh, this doesn't look good. Now, Bill, you wrote down that the perfect romantic evening is to eat a home cooked meal and watch a DVD."

"That's right, it's our favorite thing to do." Bill grinned and put his arm around his wife's shoulders. But she merely frowned back at him and crossed her arms.

"Well, it will surprise you to hear this, but Edie says her idea of the perfect romantic evening is to have dinner out and then go to a movie." The announcer tsked theatrically at the couple.

"A movie? Why, we haven't been to a movie theater for ten years. Don't need 'em when you have the DVD player."

His wife narrowed her eyes. "I like going to the movies. I like popcorn and Jujubes, and I especially like eating a meal I didn't have to cook." She pushed his hand away.

He merely gaped at her, clearly shocked to learn she didn't share his love of her own cooking and their TV room. There was a moment of dismay among the onlookers, but fortunately, the announcer quickly moved in to smooth things over.

"By the looks of you, Bill, she must be a fine cook, indeed." This brought chuckles from everyone, as the husband was indeed a bit on the large side. Even he patted his stomach and nodded.

The M.C. continued, "What do you say, Bill? Can we get a promise from you to take Edie out when you get back home?" The M.C. held out his hands, palm up, to the crowd. "How about a little encouragement for Bill, folks?"

The audience obliged with cheering, Steve and Nina hooting and hollering with the rest. Proving he was a good sport, Bill went a step beyond the request, and promised to take his wife out at least once a month. The crowd roared its approval.

Over the next half hour, promises of one sort or another were extracted from several more couples, each drawing increasingly loud laughter. The noise created by the hilarity drew other passengers to the area.

Finally, the announcer said, "Okay, folks, now we have our last couple, Steve and Nina Tabor. Where are you, Steve and Nina?" He made a show of shading his eyes as he peered out at the onlookers.

Nina, always the free spirit, gaily waggled her fingers at the M.C. Steve didn't exactly care for being the center of attention, but played along with a casual wave.

"Okay, you two. Come on down here, front and center." Hands on his hips, the announcer put on a mock stern face.

"Oh, no," Nina squeaked, glancing at Steve. "We must have gotten the worst score. I hope Grams isn't here." She searched through the crowd as she and Steve walked toward the stage area.

The microphone appeared in front of their faces. "How long have you two been married?"

"Not long enough," Steve hedged. He didn't know if Grams was out there, but he had just spotted his brother and Sandra. Damn! There was Grams right next to them. Even worse, his brother seemed to be talking to the older woman.

"Well, I don't know how long is long enough, but I have to say you two have done something no other couple has done in all the years I've been hosting this game."

A low moan told Steve that Nina had also spotted her grandmother. Oh, well. It was time to get the truth on the table, anyway. "Just how bad did we do?"

"Bad? No, you don't get it. You two each got a perfect score! Let's have a great big hand for our most compatible couple."

Nina gasped. A perfect score? How had that happened? She gaped at Steve as the cruise employees threw handfuls of confetti on them. The audience went wild with cheers.

He'd impressed her many times the past few days with his ability to glide through their masquerade, but how in the world had he pulled off this one? The list of questions had included very personal details—details about aspirations and desires. Things like how many children she wanted.

How could he have known that she thought three was the perfect number of children to have? He knew she didn't ever want to get married, so how could he guess she sometimes fantasized about being the mom of two little girls and a boy? And the questions about fantasies—well, okay, she'd mentioned her interest in feathers, so she could see how he might have guessed that one. But still . . .

As the M.C. bussed her cheek and clapped her perfect companion on the shoulder, Steve cast a wink at her. They were presented with a plastic trophy of an embracing couple. Then, with much fanfare, they received a certificate for a free dinner at the restaurant billed as the most romantic in Juneau. After posing for a photo, they were finally free to join the dispersing crowd.

Grams and the tall man joined them immediately.

"Hey, way to go, Bro." Winston patted him on the back.

Bro? Nina snapped her mouth closed. What now?

"Nina, this is my brother, Winston Tabor. You didn't really meet the other day."

"How do you do?" she said in a strangled voice. She shook the proffered hand, wishing she could sink into the deck and disappear forever. The jig was surely up now.

But no denunciation, no denial of the marriage issued from her "brother-in-law's" lips.

"I've just been talking to your grandmother, my dear. You certainly come from a talented family." He smiled warmly at her. "I am thrilled to welcome you as a Tabor."

"Oh, aren't Grams' paintings great?"

"Not just your grandmother, although I know for a fact my father bought the original she did of the cows as a hockey team. And I understand you have a sister who's a sports fashion photographer. And your parents were Olympic medalists? Dad would love your whole family." Winston clapped Steve on the back again. "I can't wait to tell him." He giggled.

"Oh, well, thank you." Nina glanced at Steve sideways. Was his brother always so effusive?

"What's gotten into you? You're acting like an idiot." This complaint came from Sandra, who'd been pouting silently beside the elder Tabor brother. "She's nothing special. I mean, just look at how she dresses." A languid hand lifted to smooth her flawless hair, managing at the same time to emphasize the drape of her designer sun dress.

Nina resisted the urge to cross her arms in front of her simple tee shirt and shorts.

"You probably don't believe this, Sandra, but clothes don't make the woman." Winston smiled with glee at Nina. "Not that you don't look sweet, honey. Just the way a writer should look." He wandered off, chatting with Grams, with a sulking Sandra bringing up the rear.

"Your parents were really Olympic medalists?"

Startled, she turned back toward Steve. He was staring at her in bemusement. "Well, yes, of course. My mother gave skating up though. After she got married."

"Nina, didn't it occur to you to tell me this earlier?"

"Well, no, not really. Why should it?" She narrowed her eyes at him. "Besides, I did tell you my parents were skaters. At the coffee shop. But you told me to cut to the chase. Anyway, does it matter?"

Chapter Nine

Any lingering doubt he might have had that he loved her drifted away with those words, "Does it matter?"

Anyone who knew anything at all about the Tabor family—or had any interest in marrying into the Tabor money, certainly knew how important sports were to the old man. Any of the society girls at whom his father had constantly thrown him would never have passed up a chance to brag about the accomplishments of their famous relatives. They'd have rammed it down his throat every chance they got.

But to this woman, it truly didn't matter. She couldn't care less if the old man would approve of her or not.

Of course, she had no interest in him, either. A sobering thought. "You're right. I can't think of any reason to have told me."

Her gaze had shifted to the disappearing trio, but she turned back to him suddenly. Slapping him lightly on the arm, she asked, "And speaking of not telling things, how come you didn't tell me your brother was on board? I nearly had a heart attack when you introduced him. Did you tell him the situation and ask him to play along?"

"Err, no. I didn't tell him." He shrugged. "By the way, he is Sandra's fiancé."

The eager light left her eyes, replaced by horrified compassion. "Oh, my. Your own brother? Wow, is that even legal?" Her hand found his, and squeezed gently. "I'm so sorry."

He shrugged again. "I'll bet my brother is too. As far as he knows, there are plenty of good healthy sports genes available to jump in the family pool now."

That seeming non sequitur earned him a blink. "What?"

A chuckle escaped him as he shook his head. He dropped a kiss on the pert nose turned up in the air solely because she had to lift her face to look at him, and then said, "Let's celebrate."

The gentlemanly solicitude with which Steve helped her over the gangplank made Nina realize yet again how easily she could grow used to traveling with a companion.

The previous twenty-four hours or so had been heaven on earth. For a change, they had dined alone, at a table set up on their balcony. Then they'd danced the night away. Steve had kissed her tenderly when they'd turned out the lights, and then wrapped her in his arms and held her close all night.

It had taken all her willpower to resist acting on desires she'd never even known she could feel.

In the morning, they'd gone on the helicopter excursion of the area surrounding Juneau, and he charmed her grandmother and sister anew at lunch. Afterwards, he had insisted she spend the afternoon in the ship's spa, treating her to a massage, pedicure, manicure—the works.

And now they were headed for the romantic dinner that was their prize for being the perfect couple.

In all, he had been a wonderful companion. Her perfect companion. But the reminder of the game they had won brought her to a sudden stop in their walk along the marina.

"Hey, wait a minute. Just how did you manage that, anyway?"

One brow rose as he cocked his head at her. "Manage what?"

"Those answers yesterday? How did you manage to get them all right?"

His lips curled in that tender way that made her toes do the same. "Funny. I was wondering how *you* managed to get them all right."

"Oh." She mulled this over. "It wasn't a trick?"

He shook his head, then nodded toward the street ahead of them. "I think that romantic restaurant is right down here."

But she merely stood and stared at him. Could the two of them possibly be so compatible? What did it mean?

She feared she knew. This man was perfect for her. In fact, it was beginning to seem more and more like fate had brought them together.

But she didn't want fate playing with her life. She was very happy, thank you very much, with her career. No man. No husband. No responsibilities. No marriage.

"Nina?" He held his hand out to her.

She hesitated, then gingerly joined her hand with his. But the heat that slid all too quickly up her arm made her pull back. Her every nerve ending seemed on alert, as though she expected disaster to strike at any moment.

But then again, maybe it already had.

Wasn't love disaster? Didn't it spell the end of a woman's dreams? Some of her dreams, anyway?

No, wait. Of course, she wasn't in love. In lust, maybe. That's all. And that's all he felt for her. Because he had made it very clear that he was out of the husband business. In fact, all this attention was surely just a prelude to the seduction he'd pretty much admitted he'd planned from the start.

Except that thought didn't seem as comforting as it should. In fact, it seemed downright disturbing.

Snap out of it. What was wrong with her anyway?

"What's wrong?" His gentle voice echoed her thoughts. "Aren't you hungry?"

Hungry? Yes, that was it. She was hungry. Starved, in fact. That's all. She could not, would not have fallen in love. With a muttered "nothing," she fell into step beside him, but kept her arms crossed in front of her.

The "most romantic restaurant in Juneau," the

Breakwater Inn, turned out to be located in a rather ordinary-looking hotel. They exchanged glances.

A frown creased Steve's brow. "Let's go somewhere else. Somewhere nicer. It doesn't seem very romantic to me."

Not romantic was exactly what she wanted. "It's probably better inside." Carefully, she added, "Anyway, we don't need a romantic spot."

He looked down at her. "Actually, I think we do. But I'm willing to give this place a look."

He started up the stairs toward the door. Mouth agape, Nina scrambled after him.

The interior of the restaurant was, indeed, a vast improvement over the hotel's exterior. In keeping with the outdoors theme that dominated most Alaskan tourist attractions, the walls were paneled in a rich, honey-colored rough hewn wood. Snowshoes, skis, and fishing equipment adorned the walls. Iron lanterns, lit with low burning flames, graced the tables.

Not romantic in the hearts and flowers sense, but rather like a mountain cabin. Exactly the sort of thing to appeal to the young outdoorsy types who adventured to Alaska. Nina liked it. Steve merely narrowed his eyes in the dim lighting.

The ski lodge atmosphere disappeared when the hostess seated them at a window looking out on the bay and marina. The late evening sunlight gleamed on the water, while brightly colored sailboats floated gently to and fro.

"Well, that's more like it." Satisfaction laced Steve's voice. He gestured toward the window, "Gorgeous, huh?"

"Hmm, yeah." But Nina's attention was more taken with her companion than with the breathtaking view. Without her own troubled thoughts to distract her, she realized how much care he had taken with his appearance that night.

Always an impressive sight, he appeared a virtual god dressed in a deep blue sport coat. She didn't know much about designers, but she suspected a very expensive one was responsible for the cut that draped expertly across those broad shoulders. The smooth blue silk of his tie, stark against the pale gray of his shirt, lent a wild stormy cast to his eyes. Or maybe it was the reflection of the fire from their lantern that made his eyes dance so wickedly at her.

Was the time finally right? Was that why the air seem to crackle around them? Was it seduction he planned?

What would she do? What should she do?

As soon as the waiter brought water, Nina took several swallows. Really, who would have thought such a tiny flame could yield so much heat? She fiddled with her silverware, arranging and rearranging the pieces, while Steve ordered wine.

When the waiter walked away again, Steve took her hand, stilling her nervous movements. "Can't you sit still?"

All her life, she'd heard a similar question, usually spoken with exasperation. But in his voice, she heard only tenderness. She smiled, even as she wondered why she felt like crying.

His fingers stroked hers, sending waves of heat up

her arms and throughout her body. But when she tried to pull her hands away, he held fast to her left hand.

Touching the stones in the engagement ring he had given her, he spoke softly. "This ring almost looks as though it was made just for you. The emeralds match the color of your eyes perfectly."

"It's very beautiful."

At his chuckle, she realized the compliment she'd given herself. She stammered, "I mean—"

His finger to her lips silenced her. "It is beautiful. But it doesn't do justice to you."

"Oh." She couldn't think of anything else to say. The warmth from his touch was now pooling in her middle, making her feel hot and bothered, and somehow, warm and fuzzy too. She waited to hear what he would say next. The fire in his eyes intensified. An answering fire stirred within her.

"As lovely as this ring is, I'd like you to wear it on your right hand."

"Huh?" She wasn't sure what she had been expecting, but it wasn't that. "Why do you want me to switch hands for the ring?" She tried to pull her fingers free from his grasp, but he held on firmly.

"Don't get me wrong. It's a very nice ring. But you deserve something created just for you. Something we didn't choose from a discount diamond outlet."

"Well, that's sweet, but after all, we only got this ring for a week." She couldn't believe he was worried about the ring now, when the cruise was nearly over anyway.

"I know we only meant for this ring to last this

week." He swallowed. "That's another reason why maybe someday, you'll accept another one from me."

His grip on her fingers tightened, but instead of wincing, she found herself holding for dear life.

"Nina, we have to talk about this pretend marriage of ours. I'd like you—"

A screech resounded through the room. Nina gasped, and jerked her hand away, knocking her glass over the side of the table.

"How could you?"

Nina's eyes widened in horror. She had not even noticed the tall blond standing next to their table. The tall blond who now had a huge water stain down the front of her silk sheath.

Nina jumped up, brushing a napkin against the other woman. "I am so sorry, Sandra. I was startled, and didn't see you, and, and . . . well, I'll pay for the cleaning, of course." Closer examination of the dress made her wince. The fabric was watered silk, which pretty much meant water would ruin it. Had ruined it.

"Get off me, you stupid cow." Sandra pushed the napkin away. Pointedly turning from Nina, she repeated her question to Steve. "How could you pretend to be married to this ditz?"

"What I do is not your business, Sandra. Not anymore. Not for a long time. And since I am thinking of making the pretence a reality, I don't know why you even think you have a reason to complain." His voice raised ever so slightly. "And she's not a ditz!"

Steve's tone sent a shiver of ice down Nina's back. He hadn't raised his voice much, not nearly as much as

Sandra had raised hers, but the set jaw and clenched fist told her he had barely kept his temper in check. The icy tingle slowly gave way to a warmer feeling. "Ditz" was a noun she'd heard applied to her more than once. But Steve had defended her.

But his ex-wife didn't seem to care. "Is that so? And this Olympic skating story you concocted for your father? That's just soooo convenient, isn't it? There's more manure in that story than in all of Texas. I can't believe you thought you'd get away with it."

"Well, not that it matters, but why would I lie about who my parents . . . ?" Nina's bewildered question trailed off in the face of the total lack of interest displayed by the irate woman.

"I don't care what you believe." Steve slammed the napkin down and rose from his chair.

"Excuse me, is there a problem here?" The hostess couldn't quite hide her nervousness, but the beefy young man in a cook's apron standing right behind her looked menacing.

"No problem. This lady was just leaving. Nina, sit down, please."

Nina sat, studiously ignoring the stares of the other patrons. Steve sat too.

"I'm not leaving until I get an explanation." Sandra pulled over a chair from a nearby table and also sat.

An elderly man at the table from which she grabbed the chair protested, "Excuse me. That's my wife's chair."

Sandra snapped at the hostess. "Get another chair for that table. And get me a drink. A double. Gin. Straight up."

Steve hissed, "Sandra, so help me, you can leave under your own power, or—"

"No, please. I don't mind explaining." Nina nodded at the other diners, still watching with concerned looks. "It's better than ruining everyone's evening."

He started to argue, but she reached over and pressed his hand. "Please?"

After a lengthy exhalation, he gave a short nod.

"Where's that drink?" Sandra's voice was still high-pitched enough to threaten every glass in the place. The waiter brought the wine they'd ordered earlier, and also a highball glass. The latter stayed where he set it for less than a second, before it was snatched up and drained. "Bring me another."

"Oh, dear." Nina had a feeling that hadn't been Sandra's first drink of the evening. "Maybe you should slow down."

"Maybe you should start this explanation of yours. And it better be good, honey."

"Okay, okay. Keep your voice down. There's really no need to get so upset." Quickly, she explained her need for a temporary husband. She finished, "And Steve has been so sweet, so perfect."

Icy blue eyes stared back at her with a speculative gleam. "So, this grandmother of yours. She's rich? You have to be married for her to put you in the will, is that it?"

"No, that is not it." Steve cut in, disgust dripping from his voice.

"No, of course not." Nina couldn't help feeling a tad insulted at that suggestion. "It is just that Grams was sick when I first told her, and thinking I'd gotten married cheered her up. I don't want her to die."

"Oh, of course not. Let the old bag live forever. But when she does kick the bucket, you'd rather she left everything to you instead of that mousy little sister of yours, am I right?"

"No! And Grams isn't rich, not really. She has a comfortable life, but she's not a millionaire or anything. And naturally, Ana and I would share her estate." Really, the insults this woman dished out were becoming beyond annoying. "And my sister is not mousy."

"Yeah, right. Look, I'm a reasonable person." Sandra ignored Steve's snort. "I won't interfere with your plans with Granny, if you just let Steve's father know the truth." A smug smile curved her bright red lips. "And you must be giving Steve a cut, so of course, you'll need to make a small deposit into my account. That's only fair, all things considered."

Nina sat back in her chair, stunned by this proposition. With an effort, she snapped her jaw shut. This woman was blackmailing them! How had her little tale of a romantic elopement ever developed into this tangle? And what in the world did Steve's father have to do with it?

"What's your point, Sandra? Okay, so Nina and I aren't married. I doubt Grams cares about that. She just wants Nina to have someone who loves her. And now she does."

Nina turned to look at him. "Loves?"

"Yes. Loves." He reached out and pulled her hand close. "That's what I was trying to say to you before we were interrupted."

She whispered, "But, you don't want to get involved. Remember?"

"I hadn't met the right woman when I said that." He stroked her wrist, sending shockwaves of pleasure up her arm. "I'm ready to give it another try."

"Oh, very touching, Steve, dear. But are you really willing to go that far to get back in your father's good graces?"

For a moment, it had seemed to Nina as though Sandra had disappeared—that the whole world, except for Steve and her, had disappeared. But those words caused both of them to turn to the spiteful blond.

"What do you mean?"

"What are you talking about?"

They spoke simultaneously, Nina curious, while anger laced Steve's voice.

"Why, didn't Steve tell you? His father is so obsessed with anything related to sports that he's likely to forget all about disowning Sir Galahad here if he looks like he's bringing some good healthy sports talent into the family. Frankly, I wouldn't even care, since there's plenty of money in that particular pie. But your little story has convinced Winston that he doesn't need to marry me and my Olympic medal." She tossed off the last of her drink. "I have to hand it to you, Steve. You certainly played this one well. I never thought telling you about my engagement to your brother would result in this." With those words, she rose. Perched unsteadily on her three-inch heels, she swayed toward the exit.

Nina and Steve, along with all the restaurant diners,

watched her leave. A collective sigh of relief was heard when the door closed behind her. Turning back toward Steve, Nina reached nervously for her wine.

Again he caught her hand. "That's not exactly how I wanted to tell you I was falling in love with you. Shall I try again?"

"Please, don't." Her voice broke with the words. She didn't want to hurt him, but how could she explain her career was her whole life? "I, I just can't."

She heard his sharp intake of breath.

"You don't believe what she said, do you? Listen, I don't need my father's money. My grandfather left me millions, and I rarely touch it." The flint had returned to his eye. "In fact, the only time I've really tapped into the trust fund for years, is for your ring and paying for that damned suite."

"Oh, no. I don't believe . . . what? Millions?" She had sagged in her chair with the weight of her misery, but now sat up straight. She knew the Tabors were wealthy, but millions? For just one of them? She was having difficulty processing all this unexpected information. She latched on the one fact most significant to her. "You paid for the suite?"

"You were worried about your grandmother paying for it. Believe me, it barely made a dent in my bank account."

She bit her lips and smiled at him. "Oh, that's so sweet." She took another swallow of her wine. "Wow. And I thought you agreed because I promised you a free cruise. I sure didn't live up to my end of the bargain, did I?" Tears filled in her eyes. "You helped me because you're a nice guy. That was your only reason."

Her tears seemed to discomfit him. "If my being a nice guy will make a sunny optimist like you cry, let me reassure you. I had every intention of jumping your, err, I mean, of seducing you."

She had to laugh a bit at that, even through the tears. "I never cry," she said, batting the moisture away. "Oh, Steve, I am so sorry. I never meant for you to be hurt in any way."

"I see." Now he took a large swallow of wine. "You're telling me that you can't return my feelings."

Unable to meet his eyes, she nodded. Yes, she supposed that was what she was telling him.

It wasn't true, of course. She was too tempted to jump over the table and into his arms for it to be true. But if she did what her heart told her to do, if she fell in love with him, she'd have to give up everything she loved.

Well, okay, not everything. Because she'd have him. But she'd have to give up her career. And she'd resent him for that, just like her mother resented her father.

And really, the fact that he was rich just made it worse. There was no way a wealthy man would want her to continue her career.

So better to just pretend she didn't love him back. They'd both be less hurt in the long run. She whispered again, "I'm so sorry."

His face had become shuttered. Voice brittle, he said, "No, don't be sorry. It's not like you didn't warn me." He picked up his menu. "We never did order. What looks good to you?"

You do, her heart screamed.

But she couldn't let herself tell the truth. "I'm really not feeling very hungry, after all. Maybe we should just go back to the ship?"

The walk back to the ship was accomplished in total silence. Guilt positively oozed from Nina's pores.

Steve supposed a good sport would keep reassuring her that she had no reason to feel guilty, but he wasn't feeling much like a good sport. He'd been so sure they were perfect for each other, that he'd found a woman who would never hound him to play society games, or badger him to give up his veterinary practice. And not that it was really important, but if his father's obsession could be satisfied in a harmless way, how perfect was that?

But somehow, in these last few days of playing houseboat, he had missed the fact that she wasn't as swept up as he was.

Yet, he'd been sure she returned his feelings. More certain of it than anything in his life. Her physical response whenever they kissed must mean something to her. What's more, they could talk for hours without running out of things to say. And they could sit in silence together and not be uncomfortable. Or bored.

They had even won that blasted contest, for Pete's sake.

So what was holding her back? It had to be something.

What had she said when they met? Her career meant more than anything? Could she think he'd hold her back? Hell, no one knew better than him the importance of doing the work you loved.

Studying her downcast eyes, he made a decision. He wasn't giving up, not yet. Maybe he'd simply rushed her. Spoken too soon. Maybe she just needed a little more encouragement. Reassurance that he'd never interfere with her job as a writer. Maybe this wasn't over yet. After all, they still had another night on the ship.

A gentleman might offer to find other accommodations, but he wasn't feeling much like a gentleman, either.

Their happiness was at stake.

He put his arms around her waist as they climbed on board. She made no attempt to move away. Instead, if anything, she leaned against him. Her acceptance gave him hope.

Arriving back at their cabin, she sat on the tiny sofa in the sitting room. He sat too, mulling ideas over in his head, letting his thoughts slip more than once to the contents of that very interesting basket.

Vaguely, in the back of his mind, he noted that the ship was leaving port. Still they sat. Nina looked morose.

He schemed.

"I am going to tell Grams the truth." Her words interrupted his plans.

Damn. Was she going to offer to sleep with her family? Carefully, he said, "I know I've said you should do that from the start, but you needn't do it just because of what I asked."

"No. It's not that." She leaned back against the dainty sofa back and stared at the ceiling. "I mean, it is, in a way. I never meant to hurt anyone, but look what my exaggeration . . . I mean, my lie, has led to. I've hurt you, and Sandra, and oh, who knows what other chains of events have been kicked off by my, my deceit." She burst into tears.

"And see. I never cry. Never. But this is the second time today!" She ended on a wail.

"Hey, no need for tears. I'm okay. It's okay. And trust me, Sandra will land on her feet." He pulled her into his arms. "Oh, honey, you meant well."

" 'The road to hell is paved with good intentions.' That's what my father always said. He said it in Russian, but it's the same thing." She sniffed. "He was right. I feel like hell."

Steve couldn't resist a chuckle as he pulled out his handkerchief. Things were looking better and better. Now, how to convince her that the hellish feeling could go away easily?

"Hey, quit feeling so guilty." He dabbed the tears from her eyes. "Believe me, the only thing you did to Sandra was keep her hands off my brother, and ultimately, my father's bankbook. I'm sure the lost prospect hurts, but she'll find someone else. And she's right about my brother. He only wanted her to please my father and keep his pockets filled."

She took the cloth from his hand and blew heartily. "But what about you? I feel so bad." She held out his hankie.

"Oh, I'll be okay." Manfully, he accepted the damp handkerchief back and slipped it into his pocket, noting with faint relief that this reassurance did not exactly cheer her up. "Although, I must say, I was really looking forward to all those homecomings. Absence makes the heart grow fonder, you know."

"Homecomings?"

Bingo. The suspicion in her voice confirmed it. She didn't think he'd want her to keep writing. Innocently, he said, "Sure. You'd have to keep traveling, wouldn't you? Otherwise, how could you keep doing your column? Sure, I'd come along when I could, but even if I hired an assistant, I probably couldn't make all your trips. So then we'd have your homecomings to look forward to." He leered at her. "That would definitely keep the spice in our lives."

She cocked her head at him, considering his words. "But what about child—"

Her question was interrupted by a loud pounding on the door. After a brief exchange of glances, he stood and went to open the door.

"Steve, Nina! I'm so glad I found you!" Ana burst into the room. "Oh, Steve. Your brother is in the doctor's office. Sandra hit him in the head with a wine bottle!"

Trust Sandra to screw things up again!

He followed the sisters as they ran towards the ship's infirmary. He had no doubt his hard-headed brother would be just fine.

Chapter Ten

In the elevator ride down to the infirmary, Ana briefly described the scene that had occurred in the dining room. Winston had just been sitting down to a late dinner with her. "And you know, Win's really kind of charming. Sort of like a playboy out of a fifties movie."

Win? Nina couldn't help but be distracted by this. Ana and Steve's brother? This was the Cary Grant type she had met?

"So what happened?" Steve asked.

"So Sandra came in. Well, stumbled in, actually. She'd been drinking. And she had this huge stain down the front of her dress, that looked like she had, well, you know."

"Oh, we know." Steve grinned, but Nina frowned at him.

"Anyway, she started yelling at me to admit that Papa

and Mom hadn't been Olympic medalists." Ana shook her head. "I don't get it. Why would someone make something like that up? What difference does it make to anyone else if they were?"

"Long story," Steve sighed. "But you're right. Only a demented person would think anyone would make up a story like that."

Nina shushed him. "She had a terrible disappointment, you know. I am sure that's why she was so upset."

"Well, maybe," said her more forthright sister. "But when Win asked her to lower her voice, she just picked up the bottle of champagne and swung at him." She shuddered. "It made a horrible thunking sound."

She reached for Steve's arm and patted it. "But he'll be fine, I'm sure. He refused to leave the dining room until the ship's security had arrested Sandra. And then he walked down under his own power."

"Oh, what a tangled web . . ." Nina murmured.

"Honey, you cannot blame yourself for this." The flat tone brooked no argument, but in her heart, she knew he was wrong. She was to blame for every bad thing that had happened on the cruise.

Ana looked at them in confusion and opened her mouth. But the elevator doors opened, and they all moved down the hall.

Dr. Kendall had just placed the last stitch when Ana led them into the doctor's office. Too late, the nurse whisked a few bloody pieces of gauze out of sight. Grams murmured praise of the doctor's work.

Looking at the still gory scene, Nina hopped from

one foot to another, wringing her hands. "Oh, Winston, I'm so sorry."

"Sorry? What for? It was the damned bi—, I mean, it was Sandra who hit me." He pinched her cheek. "But you'll be happy to know she's off the boat now." To his brother, he added, "Wait 'til I tell Dad what she did. How could you have married that fishwife? Best thing you ever did, divorcing her."

"Not quite the best thing, but I'll agree with the sentiment." The elder Tabor might try to bully his sons, but he'd never countenanced anyone else touching a hair on their heads. In the face of his brother's hale and hearty appearance, Steve clearly had no qualms about showing his amusement at the situation. "I do feel compelled to point out that I never provoked Sandra to violence."

Ignoring that irreverence, Grams asked, "How was your dinner, dear?"

"Terrible! And Grams, Winston, I have to tell you the truth about something?"

"Truth?" A faint smile frown settled on Win's brow. His stitched wound lent more menace to the anxiety on his face. "Wait a minute. Are you going to tell me that Sandra was telling the truth about your parents?"

Eyes rolled in several heads.

Through her teeth, Nina said, "No, of course not. For Pete's sake, I'll send you pictures of the medals!" Her exasperation showed how tired she was of questions about her heritage.

"But they were Olympians?"

"Yes, but—"

"No buts. That's all that counts."

Grams crossed her arms. "Well, not quite everything. You may have been feeling stunned by the blow by that time, Win, but Sandra also said that Steve and Nina were never married."

"That's what I want to tell you about. You see—"

A sudden high pitched squeal split the air. "Dr. Kendall? We have an emergency. You're needed up on deck, sir."

"Emergency? What kind of emergency?"

As the doctor barked into the ship's intercom, Nina felt a momentary sense of reprieve. A medical emergency would mean the doctor had work to do. They'd have to leave. She'd rather make this explanation in more privacy, and to Grams alone first.

"A private yacht has injured passengers. They can't make it into port due to equipment malfunctions."

The doctor snorted. "These amateur sailors. Most likely they've all been drinking and just gummed up the works."

Nina pulled her grandmother and sister toward the door. "Well, Doc, I'm sure Winston here needs his rest so—" Steve hadn't needed any urging; he was right with her.

"Not so fast, Dr. Tabor. I may need you." Nina and Steve exchanged glances as the doctor turned back to his intercom. "What kind of injuries are they reporting? Can they be moved safely?"

"They think one has broken his leg. The other passenger hit her head and keeps lapsing in and out of consciousness."

"Hmm. Sounds serious. Better not move them. We'll come to them, right, Tabor?"

"You'll have to count me out of this one."

Okay. This was it. There was no escaping it now. She'd have to explain the truth right here, with no way to cushion it. She hated to hurt Grams this way. The older woman was looking from Steve to her with question marks in her eyes.

But the charade had gone far enough. She knew Steve could not risk the harm that might result if he tried to treat humans.

"Dr. Kendall, there's something you need to know." She stopped, tears starting in her eyes. "I'm very sorry, Grams. Mr. Tabor. It's all my fault. You see—"

A voice from the ship's intercom cut in. "Hey, Doc? We also have an injured seal here. He seems to be pretty sick. Can you bring something to maybe fix him up too."

"A seal? What's a seal doing on a yacht? Darn fool amateur sailors." He shook his head. "Well, I don't know if I can help a seal."

"I know I can." Steve said quietly. "Let's go." The doctor gathered a few supplies, adding a few suggested by Steve. The two men left, with Steve saying to the doctor, "There's something I need to explain to you."

They rushed out.

Nina, Grams, and Ana were left standing in the doctor's office next to Winston's examination table.

"Mr. Tabor, you should rest." The nurse quietly urged him up from the table to a bed where he could rest.

Nina heaved a lengthy sigh. "Grams, Ana, I have to tell you something."

Green eyes so like her own twinkled back at her. "Later, dear. Let's go watch your young man in action."

Not sure she wanted to put her ordeal off any longer, Nina hesitated. "We really need to talk."

"We'll talk later. I bet you don't get to see Steve practice medicine that often."

She grimaced. Well, that was certainly true.

"Go on, you two." Ana grinned as she jerked her head toward the door. "I think I'll stay here and keep Win company."

He'd been fading a bit, but perked up at that. "Why, thank you, darling. Now, tell me all about those photos of yours." He also managed, in a most charming way, to let Nina and Grams know that four was definitely a crowd.

Nina watched for a moment as her sister's dark head leaned closer to Winston's blond one. As she trudged after Grams with a heavy heart, she hoped her sister's kindling romance with Winston might prove the one good thing to come from her lies. It might help Grams get over her disappointment, too.

By the time they reached the deck, a huge crowd had formed to watch the drama unfolding on the high seas. Grams took advantage of her elderly status to insinuate a position at the rail for the two of them just in time for them to see the lifeboat carrying Steve and Dr. Kendall reach the distressed yacht.

Steve's glossy black hair gleamed in the sunlight as he climbed aboard the yacht from the lifeboat with athletic ease.

"Wow. Isn't he just too gorgeous?" A teenager standing next to them gushed.

Nina felt a tiny kernel of pride. Gorgeous was definitely the right word.

Once aboard, Dr. Kendall moved quickly to his patients, while Steve cautiously approached his. The seal was thrashing around the deck, obviously terrified. It quieted a bit as Steve slowly drew nearer to it.

"Wow, that doctor is really good with animals." Despite the distance between the ships, his caring demeanor was evident to all who watched.

Several passengers with binoculars started reporting the details of the action on the smaller boat. As might be expected, the human patients were ignored. Everyone's attention was on the injured seal.

"Oh, no, poor thing. It's all bloody." A collective moan passed through the crowd.

"But it's been moving around a lot, must not be hurt too bad," comforted another watcher.

Nina held her breath as Steve finally got near enough to hold his hand out to the seal to smell. The breath whooshed out of her as he was able to stroke the animal's quivering head. The kernel of pride surged until her heart was filled. His ability to mix compassion and competence touched her.

"Look, he's giving it some kind of shot."

"Should he do that? What if he gives the seal something that will hurt it?" A little girl close to them tugged on her mother's arm, worry written across her face.

"It's okay, honey. He's a veterinarian." Nina knelt to reassure the child. Lifting the girl so she could see over the railing better, she pointed as Steve soothed the animal. "See, he knows just what he's doing."

The child nodded.

At that moment, he happened to glance across at the ship. He raised his hand in a thumb's up sign. She waved back, touched that he thought to reassure her in the midst of the crisis.

"He's really a vet?" The girl's mother frowned at her. "I thought he was a plastic surgeon."

"No, no." Nina eased the girl back down to the deck and half-turned toward her grandmother, who seemed transfixed by the medical action. "He's a vet. And I'm, I'm a liar."

"A liar? That's a bad thing." The little girl peered up at her with solemn earnest. "You don't look like a bad person."

"She's not bad, sweetie," Grams intervened, warm amusement filling her eyes. "She only tells harmless stories to make other people feel good. And you know what, it's actually pretty funny."

Nina stared at her grandmother. "You knew?"

"Look! He's got the seal all patched up." The white of the bandage of the now sleepy seal was obvious even for those without the binoculars. A cheer went up among the passengers.

Grams clapped with all the others, but Nina still stood gaping at her. Her grandmother glanced at her. "Quite an impressive young man you have there. Have you thought of making your little fairy tale come true?"

But Nina wasn't ready to discuss the future. She wanted an explanation. "You knew?"

"Of course, I did, Nina. You are a terrible liar." She chuckled. "I mean, you've always been really bad at it."

Nina glared back at her. "So, if you knew, why did you come on this cruise?"

"Well, I thought it would be fun to spend time with you and Ana. And also that it would force you to finally admit you didn't have a husband." Grams chortled. "Imagine how surprised I was when you showed up with Steve on your arm. So he's a veterinarian. Is that how you met him? He's Sasha's vet?"

"Yes." Still stunned, she replied absently. "That is, he's just taking over for my old one who's retiring."

Gram's face lit up. "You mean he was a perfect stranger?" Sheer delight sounded in her voice.

"Yes. Perfect." Totally perfect. So perfect it hurt.

"And here he is." Grams started clapping her hands. "The hero of the hour."

Nina looked around, and realized the other passengers were also applauding as Steve and Dr. Kendall were raised back aboard the ship in the lifeboat. Her grandmother's astounding revelation forgotten for a moment, Nina joined in the cheers, pride swelling within her. He'd certainly come through in a emergency. Seals probably weren't on his usual patient list, but he hadn't hesitated to help the animal.

Steve approached the pair to tell them he was going to clean up, but he was cut off.

"Hey, Doc." Howie sidled up to them and whispered. "Do you think you could come take a look at Maxie for Jess and me? Ever since he got on this ship, he's been seasick, you know."

He looked at Nina, who smiled tremulously at him.

"You did a fine job there, son." Grams patted his arm. "We're very proud of you." She waved him off. "Now you go on and wash up and then help the little dog. Nina and I will have a late snack. We have lots to discuss."

After a searching look at Nina, who nodded, he went off, Howie trailing behind.

Nina took a deep breath. The moment of reckoning had come. Now she was going to get to hear the riot act. Well, lord knew she deserved it. She followed her grandmother in to the restaurant with the most lavish buffet.

Feeling far from hungry, Nina chose a simple salad, while her companion filled her plate with a bit of every-thing before they found seats. Nina waited for her grandmother to finally admit her disappointment in her.

"So, tell me. When are you and Steve really getting married?" Grams took a big bite of shrimp.

Oh, no. That's why she wasn't upset. Grams thought there was something between Steve and her. For a wicked moment, Nina considered trying to pretend— no, she wasn't doing this again.

"Grams. I'm sorry. But I just can't give up my career."

"Humph." Grams narrowed her eyes. "You know, Nina, you are so like your mother sometimes, it brings a tear to my eye.

"Like Mother?" Nina stared openmouthed. "How can you say I am like Mother?"

Gram finished chewing the large bite of ham she had

taken. She gestured at Nina's plate. "Here we are, with hundreds of choices, yet you settle for a Caesar salad. It's like that line from the movie *Mame*. How does it go, 'Life's a banquet but most poor folks are starving to death.'"

"It wasn't poor 'folks' but some other word entirely." Nina had expected to hear recriminations during this conversation, but not about her menu choice. "And I am not starving to death. I just happen to like salad."

"Hmm. Melanie was much the same. She just couldn't accept that a person could take more than one choice." Grams shook her head as she managed a large mouthful of Waldorf salad. "In fact, I remember having lunch with her when you were about three months old. I asked her when she was going to return to skating."

Mother? Return to competitive skating? "I never knew she considered going back."

"Well, I don't know if she considered it. I know *I* thought about it for her. But she said she couldn't, because she was a wife and mother now."

Nina leaned forward eagerly. Here was her opening. "You see, Grams, that's why—"

"I'm sorry to keep interrupting you, dear, but I don't think you are getting my point." Grams took a bite of quiche. "Much as I hate to say it, Melanie was a fool." She shook her head.

Nina choked on a crouton. "Grams!"

"Let me finish. I'd like to think I only raised one fool, so maybe there is still hope for you. Melanie was a brilliant skater. Absolutely exquisite on ice. She was also the wife of your father's dreams, and a wonderful mother to you and Ana. She could have been all three at once, and many things more. But she just didn't believe she could skate and still love and take care of her family.

"You're too much like your mother, Nina. Life's a banquet, and you're eating lettuce." Her grandmother stood, preparing to attack the buffet again. "You've been offered a sumptuous main course, and you are turning up your nose at it. Think about that, sweetie." She headed toward the table where trays of shrimp were piled high.

Nina stared down at her plate full of soggy leaves. She looked over at the buffet that ranged the full length of the room. There were so many choices there. Why had she chosen her salad?

Of course, it's easy to take what you know. There weren't any risks that way. No fear of choosing something and discovering it's not quite what you hoped. No danger of having to get used to something new, to work at developing a taste for something.

She bit into a garlic and Parmesan coated leaf. Yes, she did like Caesar salad. But she wouldn't want to live on just salad.

She didn't have to choose just one thing. She could fill her plate with all the bounty life offered. Why hadn't she ever realized that before?

Steve embodied everything she could ask for in a mate. Sweet. Considerate. Definitely sexy. And he respected her. Wanted her to follow her path. Wanted to walk that path with her. By her side.

Why in the world was she settling for romaine lettuce, when she could have the whole wondrous meal?

She jumped out of her chair and headed for the exit.

"Finally found your appetite, dear?" Grams called to her.

"Yep, I'm starved," she tossed over her shoulder. "And I'm going to find the main course of the banquet."

Grams gave a brisk nod and a wave before she turned back to the seafood bar and loaded down her plate with shrimp and crab.

Steve was just pulling on a fresh shirt when she entered their suite. Fresh from the shower, his wet hair was plastered down on his forehead. The dark curls on his chest were still damp, and it was with great difficulty she resisted the urge to drag her fingers through the thick mat.

Eager though she had been, now that she was face-to-face with him, she didn't know how to begin. How to explain that she'd been a fool, hadn't a clue what she wanted out of life.

What if he didn't want her anymore? She searched for words.

"How's Maxie?" Darn. Of all things to come up with, she asks about a dog she's never even met?

He laughed. "As we say in the pet business, he's suffering from a dietary indiscretion."

She raised her brows.

"Apparently they've managed to smuggle him into the buffets. He's been eating too much. He just needs to run it off."

"Oh, good." She laughed. "Pretty crazy, huh? Smuggling a dog on board."

"Yep. I guess I'm glad it didn't occur to you to do the same with Sasha."

"I wouldn't do that." She grinned, amazed he'd remembered her cat's name after only one meeting. "That's totally nuts."

"Oh, wouldn't you? I'm not sure it's as nuts as making up a husband."

She hung her head. "Well, yeah. Maybe."

"How did your grandmother react to the news?" Sympathy shone in his eyes, melting her heart anew. He began to button his shirt.

"She didn't." She bit her lip, watching the progress of his fingers. "That is, I didn't tell her."

His hands stilled. "Nina, it must have been painfully obvious to everyone who saw me with that seal that I treat animals, not people." His fists found their way to his waist as he looked at her sternly. "This has to end. For your own peace of mind, tell your grandmother the truth."

Tears pricked her eyes. She'd spent her whole life being scolded and admonished by outsiders for her unconventional antics. But somehow, right from the start, Steve had never seemed to scold. He had just cared. Like now.

"She already knew." A few steps brought her next to him. She wanted him this close forever. A tentative finger touched a button. "But she said I was a fool."

"Hmm, she's a pretty smart cookie, but I don't think I agree with her on that score." His hand closed around hers. "I'm sure she just said that because she's a bit angry with you. But she loves you and will forgive you." He pulled her into his embrace and stroked her hair.

"No. I mean, yes, she does. And she was . . . illuminating." Her eyes rose to meet his.

"Illuminating?" His head cocked.

"Yes." She giggled. "And hungry. She made me finally realize how hungry I am."

He pulled back and looked down into her eyes. "Hungry? What are you talking about?"

"Life's a banquet, Steve, and I've been living on lettuce. Now I want a little bit of everything. But mostly, I want you. The main course. Every day." Her explanation done, she pulled his head down to hers.

The puzzled look in his eyes vanished as joy moved in. His lips covered hers, offering her the most sustaining nourishment she'd had in her entire life.

She would never go hungry again.

Epilogue

S*ix months later . . .*

Nina typed in the final paragraph of her article and hit the 'save' button. A few more taps on the keyboard, and the article was on its way to her editor at *21st Century Traveling*.

"All done." Snapping the lid of her laptop closed, she moved to Steve's side at the French doors leading to their balcony. Beyond the railing, a wide expanse of deep blue sea spread as far as her eyes could see. When he'd told her about the tropical beach images he'd imagined when he agreed to pretend to be her fiancé, she'd insisted they take the cruise of his fantasies for their honeymoon.

She snuggled against him as he pulled her close to his side. She definitely approved of her husband's fantasies.

Husband. Funny how that word just seemed to roll

off her tongue so easily these days. No sense of panic, no sense of being hemmed in. Just contentment. She accepted the glass of champagne Steve held up for her.

"More bubbly? I thought we finished the bottle the staff left us last night." She teased, "Dipping into the trust fund already?"

"I'd dip into it for anything your heart desired, love, but actually, my father sent this, with his best wishes." He grimaced. "Winston was sure right about his reaction to hearing who your parents were. Sorry about that."

"Hey, I am proud of them. They worked hard to be the best. And while your dad is a bit sports crazy, he's really kind of sweet." She giggled. "It's actually kind of nice to not be the most eccentric member of the family."

He laughed. "I should have known you'd find a bright side."

"But now let's be serious for a moment." He straightened and cleared his throat. Holding up his glass, he said, "Here's to success in your new column, 'Traveling for Two.'" Over the rim of the flute, gray eyes sparkled with a sweet wickedness she had come to know very well. "Although, I can't say I'm thrilled at you working on our honeymoon."

"Hey, do you know a better time to research an article about honeymoon cabins on tropical cruises?" She took another sip, wrinkling her nose at the bubbles. "Besides, it wasn't because of *my* work that we missed our first flight."

His eyes clouded. "I am sorry—"

She stretched up to kiss away his apology. "Don't be sorry. I'm just glad we were so close when the little dog was hit by the car. If you hadn't been right there, he might have died. That poor boy would have been heartbroken."

He smiled, but the troubled frown remained in his eyes. "Still, most women would be upset at having their honeymoon plans turned upside down that way. Instead of that romantic bed and breakfast in New Orleans you chose, we spent our wedding night in an airport hotel."

She took the champagne flute from his hand to place it on the nearby bureau and cupped his face with both hands. "Trust me on this, Steve. Every night with you is a fantasy trip." Her arms dropped to circle his waist, and she rested her cheek on his shoulder. "The funny thing is, you feel like home too."

His arms folded around her. A sigh of contentment escaped her as he pulled her closer.

Her gaze fell on a basket filled with assorted goodies sitting on top of the bureau, just like the one in their last honeymoon cabin. She could hardly wait to explore its contents.